The Robber and Me

JOSEF HOLUB

THE ~ ROBBER ~ AND ME

Translated from the German by Elizabeth D. Crawford

Henry Holt and Company

NEW YORK

Henry Holt and Company, Inc.
Publishers since 1866
115 West 18th Street
New York, New York 10011

Henry Holt is a registered
trademark of Henry Holt and Company, Inc.
Translation copyright © 1997 by Elizabeth D. Crawford
All rights reserved.
First published in the United States in 1997 by Henry Holt and Company, Inc.
Published in Canada by Fitzhenry & Whiteside Ltd.,
195 Allstate Parkway, Markham, Ontario L3R 4T8.
Originally published in Germany in 1996 by Beltz Verlag under the title *Bonifaz und der Räuber Knapp*.

Library of Congress Cataloging-in-Publication Data
Holub, Josef.
[Bonifaz und der Raüber Knapp. English]
The robber and me / by Josef Holub ; translated from the German by
Elizabeth D. Crawford.
p.   cm.
Summary: Because he knows that the man accused of robbery is innocent,
an eleven-year-old orphan struggles to find the courage to reveal the truth to his uncle
in their small German village in 1867.
[1. Orphans—Fiction.   2. Fathers and sons—Fiction.   3. Schools—Fiction.
4. Germany—Fiction.]   I. Crawford, Elizabeth D.   II. Title.
PZ7.H74278Bo   1997   [Fic]—dc21   97-19106

ISBN 0-8050-5599-1
First American Edition—1997
Designed by Lilian Rosenstreich
Printed in the United States of America
on acid-free paper. ∞
1   3   5   7   9   10   8   6   4   2

To K. M., in memory

— E. D. C.

Contents

On the fourteenth of March of the year 1867 the most worthy Orphan's Court of the district of Cannstatt ruled that the boy Boniface Schroll should be removed from the guardianship of his spinster aunt Wilhelmine and turned over to his uncle Emil Schroll, mayor of the village of Graab.

Here begins the story of Boniface, who lands in a remote corner of the forest, in the godforsaken village of Graab, where he makes the acquaintance of Robber Knapp and his son Christian and daughter Karolyn. And who could tell the story better than Boniface himself? After all, he experienced it firsthand!

The Robber and Me

Abandoned

I WAS SITTING UP on the driver's seat of a creaking farm cart. The driver didn't have the best manners in the world. He blew his nose into his fingers, didn't smell very good, and rarely said anything useful. I was itching to tell this beast that someone here stunk. But God forbid! A child my age could never say anything like that to a grown-up. And you can be sure, he would only be more disgusting afterwards.

We'd been under way for two days already, from Cannstatt to Graab, a village in the most remote forest, where there was supposed to be an uncle of mine.

Since my father's death I'd been living with my aunt, the spinster Wilhelmine, on Seelbergstrasse in Cannstatt. Not a particularly good life, but it could have been worse. When I think back carefully, though, life with my aunt was really more bad than good.

Aunt Wilhelmine didn't like to cook. And what a person doesn't like to do, usually she can't do well. At one swoop, she would cook enough food for four days. While a normal person like me could tolerate that to a certain extent, my aunt's knowledge of cooking was pitifully limited. She only made four dishes: bread soup, cut-up potatoes, cabbage birds, and tripe. So there was always four days of bread soup, four days of cut-up potatoes, four days of cabbage birds, and four days of tripe. Then all over again: four days of bread soup, four days of cut-up potatoes, and so forth. And that for a year and a half! Nothing else, except for a piece of bread with thin, ersatz coffee at breakfast.

So it was understandable that I wasn't as fat as, say, Carl Fuchs. But during that year and a half I did get quite a bit taller, even if not any wider. Everyone I met said I was all skin and bones.

Unfortunately, Aunt Wilhelmine had another hair-raising fault: She didn't know a thing about men. Aside from her father, there had never been a single man worth mentioning in her maidenly life. I suppose my aunt couldn't help it if she lacked all knowledge of the masculine sex. It was hardly a surprise, then, that she treated me as if my name were Boni-fac*ine* and relentlessly tried to turn me into a girl, which she succeeded pretty well in doing except for one small matter.

At some point a judge from the Orphan's Court noticed my boney frame and girlishness. Or maybe someone told him about it. The judge with the scraggly beard had person-ally investigated the troublesome situation and determined that my aunt was capable neither of feeding me properly nor of raising me to be a real man.

It was written in black and white in the civil record of the Orphan's Court that Spinster Wilhelmine's mind was "dominated by a progressive imbalance." She had too little of what was supposed to be in a normal head and too much of what didn't belong there.

The Orphan's Court had discovered that in addition to my aunt, who was completely unsuited to raising me, I had another relative. This was my uncle, Emil Schroll, who was just as closely related to me as Aunt Wilhelmine. The Orphan's Court had officially determined that this uncle was not only an upright, well-to-do, and intelligent man, but was even the mayor of a certain village of Graab, which was off in some far corner of the forest. The court decided to turn me over to him, who they believed would raise me to be a God-fearing, hard-working, virtuous Christian and a well-behaved royal subject.

How fortunate I was to have this uncle! Otherwise they would have put me in an orphanage.

God is all-knowing. He doesn't just plan for morning to afternoon but everything, far in advance. No one could ever say that God rules the world carelessly. Everything is exactly right, as it was, is now, and ever shall be.

Obviously, God also knew why I had only Aunt Wilhelmine in Cannstatt and Uncle Emil in Graab. Otherwise I was alone: no father, no mother, no brother, no sister, no one.

Carl Fuchs, who also lived on Seelbergstrasse in Cann-statt, had everything in excess: a father, a mother, two grand-fathers, two grandmothers, three brothers, six sisters, aunts and uncles, and boy and girl cousins he couldn't even count. There were so many! There were even a few in America, in Hungary, in Switzerland, and behind the Alps in Italy. God knows why He didn't give me any at all but gave Carl Fuchs so many that he didn't know what to do with them.

The one-legged beggar on the Neckar bridge in Cannstatt always said that in some people the snot simply runs up-wards. Luck usually follows the same people, he also said. It hangs on to them like a chain, but it has no time for others. It seemed that I was always one of the "others."

Even at my birth luck must have been elsewhere, because I came into the world already a semi-orphan. They said my mother didn't even get to kiss me twice.

I'd been a total orphan for a year and a half now. My father also died, and really for nothing at all. Aunt Wil-helmine had told me that in the beginning it was only a little bellyache; everyone said it could be cured with a wonder tea or a witch's brew. But the red-hot pincers didn't stop, and other sicknesses settled in and around his belly. Because of a constant lack of money, a miracle doctor was called in too late, and my father's innards were too far gone for repair.

God's ways are unfathomable. Only He knows why every-thing happened that way and not differently.

The wagon was toiling up the mountain. The driver fished into his jacket pocket more often now. He had stuck a big flask in there. He would tip a ladleful out and into himself. He already stank before, but now he also reeked of spirits.

I hoped we would be reaching this village of Graab soon. It couldn't be far away by this time.

If my father had had a little more money, perhaps he wouldn't have died. Carl Fuchs's father always had money. Every day he sold fifty loaves of bread and two hundred or more rolls. My father didn't bake bread, he taught trigonometry and higher mathematics to the merchants' sons at the Latin School in Cannstatt. He had never been able to turn his brains into money. Anyone can see that, at least in Cannstatt, it's better to sell bread than be able to do an equation with three unknowns.

The road was getting steeper and steeper. The horses were panting so that they foamed at the mouth. The driver let them feel his whip. He fished into his jacket pocket again and poured more spirits down his throat. Afterwards he belched.

Behind me, in the cart, lay all my worldly goods. In a bundle, maybe three times as big as my Aunt Wilhelmine's chamber pot, was everything the Orphan's Court had given to me: two pairs of summer pants, two shirts, a green jacket to wear to church, six stockings, three handkerchiefs, the new hymnal, my pencil, and underwear for very severe winter days. I was wearing everything else. "What he doesn't have, he doesn't need," the Orphan's Court judge with the scraggly beard was supposed to have said.

The cart was still struggling up the mountain.

Down below in the Murr Valley the meadows were already veiled in a light green; the snow was gone. But up here, in the forest, there were still dirty remnants of winter. At the edge of the road and on the north slopes, where the sun scarcely shone, snow covered everything.

Where was this village of Graab anyway?

I hoped my uncle wasn't a mean man, and I also hoped there would be something to eat besides bread soup, cut-up potatoes, cabbage birds, and tripe. Perhaps there would even be a bed for me in the house. I didn't want much more than that.

Carl Fuchs was said to get a kiss from his mother every morning. Not like the ones you got from complete or nearly complete strangers, planted on your forehead or beside your nose without any affection. A proper one. But of course an orphan shouldn't dream of anything like that. Who was there left to give me a proper kiss?

The sun had slipped down behind the forest. Its rays were no longer able to force their way through the thick branches. It was getting colder. I first noticed it in my fingers. Then I felt it in my toes, and then in my behind on the smooth-worn driver's bench. From there the uncomfortable, goose-pimply feeling crept up my spine.

Along with the darkness and cold came dread. I was often afraid, sometimes of nothing at all. Of course Father had tried to convince me from time to time that I didn't need to be afraid of anything or anyone. Fear is as unnecessary as a goiter, he always said. But that's easy enough to say. Sometimes fear slithers like a snake and stealthily settles in. Usually I didn't even know where it came from or why it was there.

There are some people you have to be afraid of. I was

tremendously afraid of God, because it's hard to be the way He wants you to be. Sometimes I was afraid of tomorrow, or afraid that I would do something wrong. When I thought about the village of Graab in the back forest, I was more than afraid. I didn't even want to think about how weird the people there were, or could be, or what kind of a strict, perhaps even mean, person my uncle might be.

At a little crossroads in the middle of the forest, the driver spat onto the crushed stone of the roadway.

"Brrrr!" he cried—with a lot of *rrrr*—and the horses responded immediately. After such miserable drudgery they were grateful to stop.

It was all right with me, too. I got down from the wagon and stretched my arms and legs, which were half asleep and therefore stiff and clumsy. My lower belly felt as if it was going to burst, and I stood to relieve myself at the edge of the roadway.

I had scarcely peed when a bundle landed next to me on the stones. My water stopped in sheer terror.

It was my bundle with all my worldly possessions. The driver looked just as sassy as ever, as if it were the most natural thing in the world for him to have thrown my belongings at my feet. Then he added very simply, as one observes that Friday follows Thursday, "That's it."

"What's it?" I asked, my water now frozen somewhere up inside. "We aren't in Graab yet, where my uncle lives. There's no village here. Only forest."

"You're right about that," said the driver, grinning. "You're right about that. This sure isn't Graab! It's just over in back. But I'm not driving there." As he spoke he waved his arms in a direction to indicate that there, somewhere amid woods and hills and ravines and who-knew-what, lay hidden this remote village of Graab.

Now I was even more anxious and frightened, and my water began to flow again.

"Dear, good man," I pleaded, "you can't leave me in this forsaken spot with night coming on so soon. It's cold, and I'm desperately hungry. I have to get to my uncle in Graab."

"Oh, yes I can!" said the driver, laughing nastily, the way a person laughs who really doesn't mean to laugh at all. "I was only paid to Sulzbach," he said. "Your uncle was supposed to pick you up there. And did he do it? No! He probably doesn't want you at all. Who'd want such a good-for-nothing snot-nose? I've brought you too far already. But this is the end of it. I'm not going to Graab; I'm going to Liedmannsklinge, and the turnoff is here. And what would I want in Graab? Or do you think I wander all over for hours on account of a little crap-in-his-pants just for fun?"

The driver stopped. He blew his nose into his fingers, which made me feel sick. Then he poured a ladleful of spirits down his throat and wiped his sleeve across his mouth.

"Graab is that way," he said, his voice sounding gravelly and boozey. "And now pay close attention to what I tell you because I don't say things twice. If you start right out and walk straight and don't miss the turnoff in the beech woods, you will soon come to Glashuette. But make a big circle around it, because there are a couple of vicious dogs there, and they're only chained in the daytime. Go around

Glashuette, and when you find the road again on the other side, go slightly upward. Only upward! Never downward! Otherwise you'll find yourself in a place you'll never get out of again. You come to four sunken paths crossing the road. Two of them are very hard to see at night. A while after the fourth there will be another, bigger crossroads. There you must no longer go straight but one quarter right. Go past the high field. However, you won't be able to see the village from the mountain. After that the road heads down gradually. After two or three thousand paces—or maybe four or five thousand—the forest ends, and Graab is in front of you. But you have to watch damn carefully to see it. There probably won't be any lights on in the village. If you have paid attention to all this, if you don't get lost, and if you aren't caught by Robber Knapp, you can be in Graab by midnight."

The driver hadn't spoken this much in two days. He spat out over the horses and cracked his whip. They started with a jolt that made the wheels spark.

The villain was gone!

The driver had abandoned me in the wilderness at the end of the world.

I stood utterly alone with my bundle at a godforsaken crossroads in the middle of the forest. The sound of the wheels on the stones grew fainter and fainter. Soon I had to strain to hear it. Some more whip crackings, then the distance swallowed the wagon. Fear descended and pressed on my chest like a mountain of stones. Cold crept into my bones, and the night slithered out of the forest from all sides and enveloped me.

Τhe Ϝorest

I SOBBED MY HEART OUT, while fear and loneliness vied to crush it.

Normally, everything on our earth is properly thought out and arranged. But there are bungles every now then. In Cannstatt, for instance, there were more people running around than you would want to see. But here in this wilderness in the remote forest all I needed was one other person—only one single person—and there was no one.

I stood there, abandoned by the world, at that accursed crossroads. The crossroads was nothing more than a gravel path with a gigantic forest in front, behind, and beside it. I prayed, implored, beseeched, and begged.

It had grown pitch-dark, and it was colder than cold. In spite of being deserted there was much activity in the forest. I heard sounds between sobs. "Is there anyone here?"

Something slipped between the trees. Probably only a

harmless animal, I hoped. Once upon a time robbers lurked near crossroads. Only long ago? The driver had also said something about a robber. Who knew how many travelers had been murdered on this very spot? Besides, there were probably all kinds of things in the forest that someone from the city, from Cannstatt, had no inkling of.

"Hello! Is anyone there?"

The cry didn't go very far. The forest closed in around my words. A gigantic bird rushed away. I couldn't see much, except for a large shadow. A vampire? Or a forest witch? Those things didn't exist! Only little children and old people believed in things like that. Didn't they?

From a great distance a bird mocked. If it was a bird! Very close by, on the other side of the road, something crept into the wilted, frozen grass. Branches clacked, and leftover fall leaves rustled.

"Is anyone there?"

A croaking, cheeky bird answered from his secure tree hollow.

I held my sobs and my breath. I could distinctly hear the panting and skulking of creatures natural and unnatural. What was there, hiding in this creepy forest?

Even the trees and bushes were moving if I looked at them long enough. I was sure that my mind was betraying me then. The more I stared into the darkness, the more the clear and normal things turned into amazingly confused forms. From nothing there arose the most intricate goodness-knows-what. If, for instance, I didn't know for sure that the dark spot beside me was a small, measly spruce,

I might think it was a crouching teeth-gnashing bear or some other monster.

"Hello!"

Why didn't God send me a passing hiker or a farmer or a peddler or a driver? Even a drunk on his way home from a tavern or a beggar would have been all right with me. It only had to be a human being.

Where was my uncle? Why hadn't he come to collect me? Perhaps it was true, what the driver said. My uncle didn't want me at all!

Something was pressing against my chest.

"Hello!"

The cry faded out, unheard among the trees. Except for the shrieking and rustling of a few startled birds or other animals, there was no answer. I was all alone in the world.

If I ever wanted to get out of this godforsaken, endless forest alive, I had to do it alone. I wiped my face dry with my sleeve. I had to look for this hidden village of Graab. I would be a coward no longer!

I started on the path the driver had pointed out to me. I hoisted my bundle onto my back and held it firmly with my right hand.

Slowly I walked in the direction he'd pointed out. My eyes had a great deal to do in the darkness. I had to make sure that I always had gravel under my feet. As long as I was walking on stones, I was on the road.

Soon I noticed a strip of light on the road. Logical. There were no trees on the road. It had to be light from the sky showing through. In spite of the dark night, the road was still lighter than the dense forest alongside.

A tiny bit of hope crept into me. Yes, I would find this village! With much care and a little luck I would make it.

Walking on the uneven, stony road was difficult. I had to feel ahead of me foot by foot so that I didn't stumble over the many obstacles. My legs were still numb and stiff from sitting, and it took a while before my muscles and joints obeyed me again.

The forest rustled and creaked. Perhaps the animals in the area were passing the word: "There's an intruder here!"

I walked on the road to Graab. The cold wasn't so bad anymore. Moving warmed me up.

I heard steps behind me. A few times I turned around. But there was nothing there. Oh, the devil take it! You could hardly see anything in this pitch-black night.

I mustn't think about what could be behind me. Who knew, after all, if there weren't still a few forgotten bears or wolves? Or maybe that robber was also slinking through the forest?

In the beech woods, which were lighter, I turned off, as I had been told. When I got careless and didn't lift my feet high enough, I stumbled over stones and gullies and holes.

Just after the turning, I stumbled over a large stone and fell full length onto the roadway. My bundle flew off in a high arc. Slowly I crawled on my hands and knees over jagged, angular stones and through muddy wagon ruts with frozen water in them. Luckily the bundle hadn't fallen into the trees.

The road stretched out into the distance. How late was it? I hoped all the lights in Graab weren't out!

I walked faster, as fast as I could. I began to count my steps. At 999 I stopped. I'd already miscounted a few times, and besides, this childish game was stupid and didn't do any good.

I heard dogs barking. That must be the vicious dogs of Glashuette. I went around the inhospitable hamlet as the driver had advised. Thank God I found the road again on the other side. I also discovered the four sunken paths. I climbed up toward the high field on the gravel road.

I went on without stopping. My legs and feet grew heavier and heavier. I wanted to sit or lie down and forget everything and sleep.

I mustn't do that! The night was too cold. I would certainly freeze, or otherwise catch my death. I had to get out of the night and out of this alien, endless, mysterious forest.

There was running water ahead of me, then beside me. Where was it coming from, where was it flowing to, and how much was there? I only heard it, and it made me anxious. It sounded eerie.

The lead in my legs was getting heavier. With each step I had to force myself to lift my foot a little higher. My heels and toes were burning inside my shoes and my legs hurt all the way up to my behind.

The road stretched on unbroken. My bundle was weighing me down. If I could just sit for a little while and let my tormented legs and feet rest. No. I must not do that. If it were summer, then I could confidently wait for morning. But it was not summer. I dragged myself on.

Where was the crossroads? I retraced my steps a little and looked very carefully.

No crossroads.

Perhaps it was still up ahead!

I stumbled on. My feet shuffled and rasped on the stones.

Then I was actually standing at a crossroads. It wasn't especially big. But there was a little track going off at a quarter-right turn. I was happy and proud, and I thought I had already accomplished the most difficult task. Now came the easy part.

Or so I thought.

Down there must be the meadow, and in the meadow the village, and in the village my uncle. Surely he had a warm place for me to sleep. Perhaps he even had a proper bed for me.

The Dream

I'D BEEN GOING DOWN for a while now. Where was the edge of the forest and the village that was supposed to be in the meadow? The forest had to end sometime! I kept walking faster, and I was surprised that I was still going along so quickly. I thought only of a bed or a bundle of straw in a warm corner.

Now that my future home lay so close, new anxieties and doubts crowded in.

What was my uncle like? I only knew him from the occasional stories told to me by my Aunt Wilhelmine. She hadn't spoken particularly well of him, but not so badly either. "Stubborn Emil," she always called him. He was a stickler when it came to law and order. The church and the town hall were the center of the village, for the gospel and the law belong together like heaven and earth. As mayor of Graab, he was stern with the community and with himself.

He practiced so much justice that it was almost unjust again, my aunt said. He had no children. Where would he get them from? From nothing comes nothing, my aunt said, and Emil didn't have a wife. No female had ever been good enough for him. She always said that the good Lord would have to make a special woman for Emil.

I could scarcely lift my feet I was so tired. I stumbled along on the path to Graab. Instead of legs there were lumps of lead dangling from my body. Only the prospect of arriving drove me on.

Meanwhile, I dreamed of a warm bed. More and more often my eyelids closed, and I had great trouble forcing them open again.

I must be way beyond the high field, for the road had been dropping steeply down for some time. A little too steep for a road! Crusted snow crunched under my feet. I had to watch out to keep from sliding. Then the road was free of snow again for a little while.

The road?

My head grew hot. What had happened to the gravel under my feet?

The road had shrunk to a narrow, slightly frozen path with ordinary forest soil. No wheeled vehicle could travel here! I wasn't on the road anymore!

I started wide awake. My heart thumped so hard against my chest with anxiety, fear, and disappointment that my ribs trembled.

Just don't go crazy now! I stopped. I must go back to the top. There was still gravel up there.

Hastily I began climbing again. I marveled again at how steep the path was. At a fork in the path it was even more difficult: I no longer knew which direction I had come from. Had I ever even *been* on one of these paths?

What was there to consider? Either path could be right or wrong. I had to decide on one of them. I would go right.

In desperation I rushed on. The air in my chest grew scant. I panted a little until the whistling in my lungs went away.

Onward! I no longer felt my feet and legs. Remnants of snow crackled under my shoes, but still no gravel. Fear of the night and this bewitched forest without end drove me on.

Why did the path suddenly stop?

Now nothing fit together anymore!

It was the wrong path.

Back!

It must have been the other path at the fork. My feet stumbled. I was sucking in as much air as I could. The pipes in my throat whistled like the old organ in the Uffkirche in Cannstatt.

Why didn't the fork reappear? It should have turned up ages ago. The path made a bend downward. It dropped away very steeply. This was also the wrong way! Back again!

All at once that path disappeared too. Accursed and bewitched!

I fell down a slope. Even farther below there was the sound of water.

Now I knew I was lost. In fear and desperation I cried as loud as I could. "Help! Help!"

What a hellish night this was!

Terrified, the animals in the forest dashed away, over last year's rustling leaves and through the whipping branches of the underbrush. The animals were afraid of my bellowing. Soon the tumult subsided on the other side of the rushing water, and then it was quiet again.

I was trembling with cold and despair.

Ice-cold clouds of mist rose from the water. They seeped through my clothing and mercilessly took hold of my skin. I pulled my Sunday jacket out of my bundle. But that didn't provide much warmth either. Would I still be alive tomorrow?

Exhaustion was creeping up on me. I could no longer open my eyes. Dreams flitted through my head. Frightening faces and monsters chased me through the forest, up and down, through icy water and freezing clouds.

Then the spooks were gone. It became almost peaceful in the forest. A big man wearing a black hat came up to me.

He took me up in his arms and carried me away, out of the eerie, endless forest. If that's what really happened. Perhaps I was already asleep.

Ħeaven

I WAS IN HEAVEN.

I must have frozen to death last night in the terrible forest.

How else could I be lying in this heavenly bed, with a thick, fat cumulus cloud piled on top of me.

Heaven wasn't blue, but it was beautifully warm and comfortable. Just like a house, there was a window, and when I looked up, I could see the sky covered with roofing panels. Well, why not? Sunbeams streamed in through cracks. Thanks be to God that there was sun in heaven. How dumb! Heaven was where it lived.

Strange! There was hunger, too. Something growled under my shirt. That must be my soul. In heaven you didn't have anything except your soul. Somewhere there was the smell of malt coffee. And I had to pee. Aha! You had to do that, too. It was almost like being on earth.

I crept out of my cloud. I had on my shirt but not my

pants. In heaven you were only supposed to be naked when you were an infant, a little angel. Otherwise not at all. This didn't fit!

My cloud looked like a big featherbed.

I went to the window. It was beautiful in heaven. Like the country. The sun was shining on a village street. There were big and small houses, with barns and sheds. The smell of dung heaps rose up to the window. It was very reassuring to find that it stank a little in heaven, too.

Somewhere in the neighborhood a powerful male voice was cursing with frightful profanity.

I was horrified. I wasn't . . . ?

Anxious and disappointed, I crept under my cloud again. I stubbed my big toe on the bedpost. The pain throbbed under my toenail.

Then it dawned on me. I was in the attic of a farmhouse.

So I hadn't frozen the night before, and I considered for a while whether that was a good thing. My uncle had found me and brought me into the village.

The garret was small. There was only a giant bed in it, with a cover that was stuffed with half a goose pen.

Curiosity drove me to the window again.

I looked out over several roofs. All the chimneys were smoking. Dung heaps steamed gently, and along the edges of the street there were shimmering brown puddles of liquid manure.

The new day was clear and clean. There was nothing fantastic or confusing anymore. The sun shone on the darkest corners and banished the secrets of the night.

Hurried steps clattered up the stairs.

A large, sturdy woman came into the room.

"Are you Boniface?" she asked. "Yes or no?"

Her voice was brassy and loud, and she reminded me of the butter woman in the Cannstatt Saturday market. I was afraid of this powerful woman. Quickly I leapt back into bed. But I wasn't safe there either. The warm, thick cover was simply snatched away.

"Are you Boniface or aren't you?" the energetic voice repeated. "Come with me, and hurry. The mayor is waiting for you!"

I quickly slipped into my pants, which were hanging on the bedpost, and sprang after the woman.

Three men and two girls were sitting around a big table. They were just having their morning meal. The room was large and everything in it was large. It had to be the kitchen, because in addition to the table there was a gigantic cook-stove built into the wall. Pots and pans hung over it on a pole. The whole kitchen smelled wonderfully of malt coffee.

Everyone was looking at me curiously.

The man at the head of the table examined me thoroughly, as if he wanted to take me apart piece by piece. I then knew that this stern face belonged to my uncle. He reminded me a little of Father.

"So you are my nephew Boniface!"

"Yes!" I risked a glance. No doubt about it. My father had the same mouth, same eyes, same eyebrows.

My uncle stared at me, too, and our eyes met for a moment.

I couldn't figure out whether or not he liked me. His face

said nothing at all. Perhaps it was his official face, his mayor's face. I hoped he had another one, too.

"Why do you look like a girl?"

"I don't know!" I was ashamed. Everyone always mistook me for a girl.

From a pot on the stove came the seductive smell of malt coffee.

"How is it that you arrived past midnight? I was supposed to fetch you in Sulzbach this evening."

My uncle's voice was stern but not cold.

I overcame my fears and shyness and recounted the entire story: of the journey, how the driver had set me down in the middle of the forest, and how I had tried to walk on to Graab alone, which, unfortunately, I had not succeeded in doing. And I did not conceal that I had gotten woefully lost. Somehow I must have fallen asleep.

"God be praised you found me and brought me to the village," I concluded.

It was as quiet as a mouse in the kitchen. Why didn't anyone say anything? I looked anxiously around the table. Did I do something wrong or say something unseemly?

"No. I did not find you in the forest," my uncle said, almost meanly, and anger drew his eyebrows together frighteningly.

I was afraid, but I soon saw that it wasn't me he was angry with.

After a while my uncle spoke, and anyone could see and hear he was furious at the callous driver: "He is going to get something he wasn't looking for! Leaving a small, ignorant city boy in the middle of the forest at night! That's more than carelessness or thoughtlessness—that's gross negligence or malice aforethought."

With a critical glance at me he added, "In the cold, you could have ended badly. You have to know your way around in our forests."

After a while he asked, "Can you remember who found you in the forest and brought you here?"

"No. I think I must have been asleep. I probably only dreamed about the big black hat."

My uncle looked around the table. "Which of you heard anything, and more important, who saw anything?"

The old man sitting next to my uncle swallowed hard twice.

"Mayor!" he began, and to me he said in an aside, "I'm the chief farmhand, Daniel.... Mayor!" he repeated. "I don't sleep so well anymore, so I hear almost everything that goes on at night. If a cow is sick, or if the hens are nervous because a fox is lurking about in the farmyard, or when my young farmhand climbs out of his window, or when the village lads stand under the maids' bedroom window ..."

The two girls at the table blushed. So they were the farm maids.

"Daniel!" my uncle broke in. "I don't want to know everything you hear when you can't sleep. I only want to know what you saw or heard last night—and, above all, who brought this skinny little bag of bones, this half-pint, to the front door."

My uncle didn't like me! What names he called me!

"That's just what I'm trying to tell you, Mayor. I heard something, but I didn't see anything."

"Yes, of course, Daniel. I heard something too. You couldn't not hear it. Half the village must have heard it. What's important is whether anyone *saw* anything!"

The woman who'd been in my bedroom before pulled at her earlobe.

The mayor asked her, "Well, Frederika, did you see something?"

Aha, the woman's name was Frederika!

It took her a while to get the first words out. "After the bang on the front door I ran to the window and looked out, and then I thought I saw someone going up the street."

"Yes, and . . . ? Keep talking! Who was it?"

"That I don't know. I only saw the man from behind, and besides, it was pitch-dark."

"How do you know it was a man if it was pitch-dark?"

"Because a woman doesn't wear a hat, and besides, no decent woman is ever running around at night when it's time to be asleep. Maybe the midwife, but she's much smaller. And besides, no child was being born last night. It was probably a poacher. He wouldn't want to be asked what he was doing in the forest in the middle of the night."

"Anything is possible. . . . Did *you* see anything?" my uncle asked in the direction of the maids and the young farmhand.

All three shook their heads. They probably slept too well. They heard and saw nothing.

The interrogation was at an end. My uncle went into a

room next door. The others also stood up and left the kitchen. Only the powerful woman, Frederika, stayed behind. She fussed with pots and added wood to the fire in the stove. The embers were very weak and so she blew on them.

I was still standing beside the table. Nobody had bothered to say anything more to me, and the smell of malt coffee coming from the pot on the stove was still so wonderful.

There was no room here for me! Why couldn't I be in heaven and stay there. No one liked me! My uncle and this woman were even worse than Aunt Wilhelmine. There was a pot of malt coffee on the stove and they were letting me die of hunger right next to it! I had simply been abandoned by God and the whole world. As far as I was concerned, every-one—including this uncle of mine—could go jump in the lake! No one wanted an orphan boy!

As I was wallowing in self-pity, the big cookstove with the pot of malt coffee suddenly began to waver. They turned around by themselves, swung up the wall, slid along the ceil-ing, and came down on the other side again. Window, door, table, and everything else in the kitchen, even this Frederika, began to swirl as well. I was standing in the middle. The en-tire kitchen was spinning. Faster and faster it all tumbled to-gether until it was just a big knot. And then it disappeared.

I was lying under my cloud. No, once again it was only the bed in the attic, and this terrible woman, Frederika, was standing next to it.

"Well, well, he's still alive!" she said with her brassy pot-lid voice.

I snapped my eyes shut again. The woman didn't like me! And I didn't like her! The devil take her! I wanted to have my rest.

Somewhere something smelled awfully good. It had always smelled like that in Fuchs's bakery on Seelbergstrasse in Cannstatt. The fragrance of malt coffee wafted around the bed. I blinked. Wasn't that a chair beside the bed and on it a pot of malt coffee? And a thick slice of bread next to it, spread with marmalade or jam? Was I not dreaming? How did I know this wasn't some kind of a trick being played on me?

The good smell persisted.

My stomach growled like a chained dog. When was the last time I'd eaten anything? It was an eternity ago. The day before yesterday. Maybe even longer.

If only this woman weren't here. She could go to blazes! She was still sitting on the edge of the bed. But then this Frederika said in a very gentle voice, "Boy, eat. You absolutely must eat. Otherwise there'll be nothing left of you!"

What a surprise! Who would have thought that this woman could also speak so butter-soft? Surprised, I looked into her face. Did she mean it seriously? She had very friendly eyes. No, she seemed to have nothing against me and my hunger.

As if she read my thoughts, she repeated insistently, "Boy, eat! Otherwise you'll collapse on me again. And it's apple-pear-raspberry jam on the bread. You won't get anything like that anywhere else. You'll only get that from me. Try a little!"

I didn't wait to be asked again. I leapt out of bed, took up the gigantic bread slice, and wolfed it down. I had never eaten such good apple-pear-whatever jam in my entire life. In between bites I drank the malt coffee with pleasure.

The sun peeped through the window, and all at once I found that life in my uncle's house wasn't so bad. But the difficult and very important question remained: How long would it stay this way? I had already had enough bad experiences. Fear was already nibbling at my small joy. Who could tell how long this Frederika would be so friendly? One thing was certain, my uncle surely didn't like me. I was a burden, or at least of no importance to him.

"Why are you putting on that ugly frown?" asked Frederika. "Are you still hungry?" She didn't wait for an answer. "Come to the kitchen with me! I have a good chicken soup on the stove. A soup like that will bring the dead back to life."

Of course I went to the kitchen with Frederika and spooned up the big plate of chicken soup she put in front of me.

My uncle came out of the adjoining room. He asked me this and that, about the Orphan's Court judges and about my dead father. He also explained why he wasn't at his funeral a year and a half ago. He'd learned of it too late. The letter from Aunt Wilhelmine had arrived two weeks after the funeral.

A man in a washed-out blue uniform with red lapels and cuffs entered the kitchen.

"Beadle and Police Constable Fuenfkorn present for morning report!" As he spoke he clacked his shoes together so hard that muck dropped from the soles. At the same time he saluted. "I respectfully beg to report that there are no unusual criminal occurrences in the district!" He further reported that yesterday at exactly one o'clock at night he had shut down the inn, the Lion, and the company brewhouses, the Stag and the Little Horse. All patrons had left. The church-tower clock continued to run three hours fast. But it should not be changed because people had gotten so used to it, and in the end it didn't matter what time the sun rose and set in Graab—the animals didn't follow the clock. And besides, they'd had bad experiences with changing the clock. The last time they tried, it wouldn't run for days afterwards.

The beadle and police constable further reported that today Gottfried Roerhle's sow had farrowed early and that all five were healthy, praise the Lord, which could not be said of old Jacob Wieland's widow, whom consumption would soon cast into the grave.

The beadle and police constable took a deep breath. You could clearly see how his lungs expanded. His forehead creased into a frown under his uniform cap. He was thinking. But apparently nothing more came to him. Thus he ended his morning report, *"Exakt!"* and then he looked at me quite curiously.

The mayor noticed and said, "This is my nephew, Boniface, from Cannstatt. He will be living with us now."

The beadle and police constable saluted and said, *"Exakt!"* and then he added a little doubtfully, "His name is Boniface?"

"Yes, his name is Boniface!" the mayor replied sharply and then asked rather quickly whether the beadle and police constable had perhaps heard or seen by what means this nephew of his had come into the village last night, or, to put it another way, who had placed the boy at his front door.

Beadle and Police Constable Fuenfkorn had no idea. "I don't know anything about this," he said. "I went right home after shutting down the pubs at one o'clock Graab time, which, as everybody knows, is ten o'clock Backnang time. And since my old woman—or, respectfully, my wife—snores as much as I do, we both hear nothing else. But I'll check around in the village. *Exakt!*" He clapped his heels together, saluted the mayor, and left the kitchen with a dignified policeman's tread.

Some odd thoughts were going through my head.

A strange village, this hamlet of Graab was. At night it hid itself in the forest, and you could hear and see nothing of it. Then when the sun came out, the hideaway glowed. Perhaps it was like that with its inhabitants too. They acted quite reserved and distant. For example, Frederika. She thundered and thumped about terrifyingly, and yet she wasn't so bad after all.

When I considered it carefully, I needn't be too unhappy. The morning meal was good. Where else would you get bread with jam on an ordinary day? And I had just been given my own room with a gigantic bed and warm covers. I hoped I could keep the bed and wouldn't have to move over when there were overnight guests. No, Frederika wasn't half bad. She'd even pushed back my hair before, and I got all red with embarrassment because it felt like a caress. I could certainly get used to her brassy voice.

Even Uncle could be worse. He hadn't done anything to me yet. Aunt Wilhelmine was quite right. Uncle was no ordinary man. He was somewhat between the ground and the clouds, though not so far as God Himself. Perhaps my uncle was something of a substitute God for the village.

Frederika asked me if I wanted to see the farm. She had a little time now, and as a future inhabitant of the house, I had to learn my way around.

"By the way," she said, "I'm your uncle's maid." She showed me the house, the barn, and the sheds. It was nice and warm in the barn. The cows were standing like soldiers in two long rows. They did nothing but eat, chew their cud, and when they lifted their tails, manure splashed on the floor. Anyone who didn't jump away in time got the green and gray-brown muck on his feet.

In a side stall there was a gigantic animal with a thick, broad head and no udder. It had a huge ring threaded through its nose. The ring was attached to a massive chain and the chain attached to the wall of the stall. With horror I realized that this gigantic animal wasn't able to move much. Otherwise the chain would pull on the ring and the ring on its nose. I shivered just thinking of it.

"Why is this big cow attached so uncomfortably to the chain?" I asked the maid. "Was she bad?"

But Frederika only laughed. "That's Hexer, our community bull. He's needed so there'll be calves. He's very wild and dangerous. So you must never go near him! But he's very good. He can mount three times in one day."

"Aha! Then he really is good!"

Of course I had no idea where or over what Hexer mounted.

The mayor was sitting in the village office.

"Psst!" said Frederika when we had gone past. "In there he's not your uncle. In there he's the mayor, and he's all business. We're never allowed to disturb him in the village office. There isn't anything important enough for you to ever enter this room without being invited," Frederika whispered. "Perhaps if the house were burning down, or if it were a few minutes before the end of the world. But I'm not even sure of that."

Frederika left to go back to her work.

I went outside. The street beckoned. There would certainly be some things to discover there. Just to the right was a pond with geese and ducks. The large, crooked willow tree on the bank offered a wonderful place for a hideaway.

Unfortunately nothing came of it. Just as I was going to climb the tree, the window of the village office was flung open, and Uncle called out, "Stop, stay where you are! What next! Mindlessly climbing around in trees! Idleness is the root of all evil. See the house with the little tower there ahead to the right? To the right, I said! Yes, that one there! That's the school. You go right down there and report to Schoolmaster Altmayer! Yes, right away! At once!"

The window was shut again.

I didn't have much time to think it over. There was nothing to think over, anyway. I sensed that two eyes were following me relentlessly. So I went straight to the house that had been pointed out to me.

The Schoolhouse

I STOOD IN FRONT of the schoolhouse.

A schoolhouse is different from any other house. It doesn't matter whether it's old or new, big or small, plain or showy. You don't just see a schoolhouse—you hear it and smell it.

A droning and coughing filled the schoolhouse in Graab, forcing its way through the windows and into the village streets.

I compared this quite modest little house with the Latin School in Cannstatt. No, they just couldn't be compared. This was something entirely different, it was pitiful.

Uncertainty pressed against my stomach area and up to my windpipe. Just don't let my knees start knocking now! They did, and it got worse. There was only one door on the ground floor. I knocked.

A small child's voice called, "Herr Assistant Teacher! Somebody knocked!"

So that was the wrong door.

Although no respectable boy would run away like a coward, I immediately leapt up the steps. I waited there a while until the downstairs door was closed again. If the assistant teacher was on the ground floor, the schoolmaster must be upstairs. Logical.

I knocked moderately, enough to be heard but not to annoy anyone.

Steps came to the door right away. A stout older man stood in the doorway. "What do you want, girl?"

"I'm a boy, and Mayor Schroll sent me. I'm to report to Schoolmaster Altmayer."

The schoolmaster looked me over several times from toe to top and top to toe. "Aha! So, a boy! But what kind of a boy!" Then he bellowed like the meanest hound of hell: "To whom are you supposed to report, boy?"

"To Schoolmaster Altmayer!"

His fearsome eyes glared at me, pounding me deep into the ground. In a cutting voice I was instructed, "That is, 'I must report to Herr Schoolmaster Altmayer,' boy!"

He bellowed the word *Herr* so sharply and loudly that it rang throughout the building. The trumpets of Jericho must have sounded like that when the walls of the city came down some thousands of years ago.

Total silence descended, even down in the lower class.

I had a huge lump in my throat and I looked at the schoolmaster wordlessly. But the man with the commanding voice of two field marshals had reckoned on that anyhow. He shoved me into the classroom.

Close, foul air crept into my throat and down into my lungs. There was barely enough air to breathe in that room. Eighty to a hundred children were sitting squeezed into much too small a space. They shifted restlessly. But when the schoolmaster banged his stick on the desk in front of him, it was instantly as quiet as a mouse.

I felt quite alone among all the children, and suddenly my anxiety was back again. But at the same time there developed in me a lump of defiance, a little courage, and curiosity.

"What's your name, boy, and where did you come from?"

"My name is Boniface Schroll, and I come from Cannstatt."

Subdued *Ah*'s and *Oh*'s and a soft giggling rustled through the class. Was it the girl's hair or the name Boniface or because I was named Schroll or that I came from so far away?

"Are you related to His Honor the Mayor, boy?"

"Yes, he is my uncle!"

"Aha! So, so! How old are you, and what grade were you in in Cannstatt, boy?"

"Eleven and a half years old, and I was in sixth grade at the Latin School."

"Aha! So, so! Then you will remain here in the upper class, boy!"

The boys had to squeeze together, which was almost impossible, because it was already much too crowded.

"Carl Weber two! Make yourself thinner!" cried the schoolmaster.

I squeezed into a tiny gap between two boys in the third row of benches. I couldn't move, and I thought I was going to suffocate. Both my neighbors shoved and pushed. The schoolmaster banged his stick on the desk and the shoving stopped.

I thought longingly of the Latin School. There wasn't a single girl there, and there was one bench for every four boys. Each could sit comfortably without touching his neighbor. The teacher walked back and forth between the rows of benches. How would Herr Schoolmaster Altmayer ever do that? He would have to climb over benches and pupils when he wanted to keep a close eye on the back-benchers. But as I found out, he didn't need to do that. He stood in front, like General Napoleon, and directed the class from there with his stick.

"We will continue!"

In the second row a girl with a long, brown braid stood up. How long was her braid? Too bad I couldn't see the whole thing. Did it reach to her behind?

"Ow!" A neighbor pinched me in the buttock, and someone else pulled my hair. I tried to report it to the schoolmaster. But that brought no comfort. The rogue next to me put on the most innocent face in the world, and the wretch behind me pretended to know nothing about it.

The girl with the long braid recited a little verse, something holy-sounding. Her voice was clear and soft. Probably it was a verse from the hymnal. In Cannstatt we never did anything like that. I carefully asked my other neighbor, "What's she doing?"

"We're having memorization drill."

"Aha!"

Herr Schoolmaster rapped his stick on the desk so that all the boys and girls jumped. "Quiet!" he thundered, and then right afterwards he said with false sweetness and calm, as if nothing had happened, "Continue."

The verses traveled along the row of girls, then they jumped over to the boy's side. The memorized verses were repeated without mistakes.

I was amazed at how perfect it all was. My jaw dropped in genuine respect. There had never been anything like this in the Latin School. I didn't quite know what to think of it. The little verses were completed without the slightest stammer. It sounded really eerie.

There was a lull. I was the obstacle.

"Continue!"

The verse tapeworm jumped over me, hopped to Carl Weber two, and slithered on to the rows behind in the prearranged order.

All at once the thread was snapped.

Some boy on a back bench caused the interruption.

I didn't notice anything. However, a miscreant must have said something wrong. The schoolmaster was furious. He beat the desk with rage.

"Repeat!" he screamed, his face beet-red.

The boy behind repeated in a strong voice. "The anger of men is not just before God."

What was so special or so bad about that? Why was the schoolmaster angry?

"Christian Knapp!" bellowed the schoolmaster. "Come here, rogue!"

His voice was as sharp as an archangel's or an executioner's. "I'll cure you of your recalcitrance, young fellow! By what right did you choose that verse yourself! If you keep on this way, boy, you'll never get on any better in life than your robber father!"

The upper class was dead silent. But up front, among the girls, there was a soft sobbing. Or was there? Yes! Wasn't it the girl with the long braid? Why was she crying?

The entire upper class was looking at the evildoer, whose name was Christian Knapp. Those sitting in front turned around so they would miss nothing.

The anger in the schoolmaster's command was hardly concealed: "Come here, villain! You parasite on the kingdom, you limb of Satan, you robber's brat! Come here, Christian Knapp!"

This was the second time I heard the robber mentioned. The driver had also warned me of him yesterday. So this was the son of the thief. The schoolmaster certainly didn't like him. Otherwise he wouldn't have reacted so viciously to his little prank.

My skin prickled from the middle of my spine down to the back of my knees. What did the son of a robber look like? Wild and brutish? Naturally very disgusting, how else? I was curious about his face. Christian Knapp crawled over desks and boys to the front. He pushed right past me. I saw his face only briefly. There were no warts or pockmarks on it. Funny, he didn't smell sulfurish like the Devil, either.

Christian Knapp stood in front of the schoolmaster, who

turned him around so that his face and chest lay on the desk. Then he pulled the boy's somewhat too large trousers tight and hit him with the stick. The schoolmaster raised his arm high so that the blows would really hurt.

"A punishment without pain is like a religion without hell!" panted the schoolmaster.

I felt sick. My heart raced. Why was I getting upset about this robber's son? What did it have to do with me, anyhow? He was getting the blows, not me. But I felt sorry for him. He was being thrashed for absolutely nothing at all. That was more than unjust. The schoolmaster was a devil. Soon Knapp would be bawling and crying. No boy's behind could withstand such blows. The schoolmaster continued beating and hitting.

Christian Knapp did nothing. No sound, no groan, not even a sigh. Hats off! Was a robber's son so hard-boiled and feelingless? Because he had the devil hidden in him? Witches were supposed to be that way too.

At some point the schoolmaster gave up beating the boy. His face was fiery and sweating, and the veins in his temples were as fat as earthworms. He stood the boy upright, and the entire upper class could see that Knapp hadn't shed a single tear.

"How can anyone be so unrepentant!" croaked the schoolmaster, out of breath.

But Christian refused to give him any satisfaction. His face was impassive. He simply wasn't in the schoolroom. The boy didn't look at the schoolmaster. He didn't look at anyone at all. Christian Knapp's eyes bored a hole into nothing.

In the girls' rows up in front, someone was still sobbing very softly. But almost no one took any notice of her.

"Recite!"

Knapp sat down again in his seat. I still see his face before me. Those eyes—beautiful, but fearful. Even if he was only the son of a robber. I was surprised to find that I hated the schoolmaster.

The boys and girls recited the pious sayings in the established order. There were no more mistakes. The verses ran down the rows as if steered by a ghostly hand. They all had to do with God, with His power, dominion, and pity, and with His boundless love for humankind.

When the Graab church clock struck three, Herr Schoolmaster banged on the desk. Now it was midday throughout the rest of the country.

"Up!"

We got up, straight and quiet. Before we were dismissed, an older girl gave thanks in our names to God, the king, and Herr Schoolmaster for the benefits received.

Shorn Like a Lamb

THE MIDDAY MEAL was a bright spot in my new life. At the mayor's house there were yeast dumplings with dried fruit. The whole kitchen smelled of them, and my stomach was doing somersaults of joy.

A good meal can work miracles, and the fact that the people in the mayor's house were content with themselves and the rest of their small world was not to be dismissed.

I sat beside Frederika. That was nice.

She asked me how the first day at school had gone.

"Oh, all right," I said, and then I looked carefully at my uncle out of the corner of my eye. His face was somewhere between official and private, and so I dared to answer Frederika honestly. "The school's horribly crowded, and the schoolmaster isn't very amiable," I replied. Then I told about young Knapp's beating, and I didn't try to hide the fact that the schoolmaster was more than unfair.

My uncle looked interested, and when I asked Frederika about Robber Knapp, he joined our conversation.

"Knapp?" he said. "There's not much to tell about Knapp. He's a bad fellow. He lives somewhere in our forests. In a cave, they say. Where? Nobody knows! Otherwise he'd have been arrested already. He makes the entire district unsafe, and he steals whatever he can get his hands on. We don't know exactly what he steals. But a robber always steals. Otherwise he wouldn't be a robber. Our forests are notorious all over the kingdom. Soon no one will dare to go through them anymore. Although Knapp is wanted by the authorities and we've sent out bulletins, he manages to avoid being caught. But sooner or later someone will get him, dead or alive. Now, if the Prussians were doing it they'd have taken him long ago!

"Mark my words," added Uncle after a long pause, "when someone takes the steep path, he slides inexorably down. The steep path is as smooth and slippery as fresh cow dung."

Old Daniel was rocking his upper body back and forth. That didn't necessarily mean anything, but it could also be that he didn't agree with what was being said. Silently, Frederika was shaking her head too. The young farmhand was pleased that the others were all caught up in the conversation. He took shameless advantage of the interruption by eating, and he took dumpling after dumpling out of the serving dish.

I didn't give up. "And Christian Knapp, the son of the robber?" I asked excitedly. "He can't help it if his father is a robber. Why did the schoolmaster beat his behind black and blue? Just because he recited the wrong verse at the wrong time. For that the schoolmaster beat him till he was just about half dead."

Uncle reflected. Then he said a little more loudly, "The son of Robber Knapp, Christian Knapp, could be quite a clever boy. But he's the son of a robber, and so it doesn't do him any good to be clever. For what purpose? Instead of being good and quiet, he's rebellious like his father. What made him mix up the order of the sayings in the recitation? It's intolerable for a pupil to interfere with the authority of a teacher. It's the same whether it's with the wrong saying or with impertinent questions. The pupil must do only what the teacher wants. The teacher asks the questions and the student answers them."

Strange, I thought, and then gathered up my courage and said to my uncle, "But in the Latin School in Cannstatt we were allowed to ask the teacher anything."

"That is another matter entirely," Uncle replied, with a wave of his hand. "Only the sons of the respectable city men go to the Latin School, and they obviously have to learn more than ordinary farm children. The farmer must work and fear God. He doesn't need to learn any more than that."

Everyone sat there thinking. Old Daniel was still wagging his torso. The dish of dumplings was empty. Too bad. I should have eaten and not talked. The young farmhand was looking at it with satisfaction. He was full of dumplings.

Suddenly my uncle said to Frederika, "Give Boniface a decent boy's haircut!"

"Oh, that beautiful hair!" wailed Frederika. "Do you want to shear the boy like a sheep?"

Uncle looked at me. His face was stern. "The hair comes off! The boy is nothing special, and he will not be treated differently. He will be trimmed like all the village boys!"

There was no contradicting that.

Uncle stood up. "One more thing, Frederika. Those short city pants must be lengthened. My nephew can't run around here like that. I'd be ashamed of him."

"What shall I lengthen them with?"

"It doesn't matter. The pants must extend over the knees. That's that." Uncle went into the mayor's office. This was a sign to the others that dinner was over. They went back to their work.

Frederika got out a huge pair of scissors. She probably used them to clip the wings of chickens and trim the horses' tails. Sighing, she turned me into a village boy. Soon there was only stubble left on my head.

"Can I look at myself in a mirror somewhere?"

"Oh, Boniface! You'd better not! You probably won't recognize yourself anymore." She took one of the curly locks and slipped it into her apron pocket. Did she collect hair?

Using the same scissors, she also cut my fingernails. She did it very carefully. I didn't know whether to laugh or cry. On the one hand, I was glad not to be a girl anymore, but on the other hand, I felt like a shorn lamb, and my head was awfully cold.

I ran out of the house. When I got outside I felt better. The afternoon sun warmed my bare skull as I sauntered through the village that was now my home. What a home! Even on the very first day it was full of surprises.

The village wasn't large. I got through it quickly. There was a single street. I counted twenty-two houses, not including the barns, sheds, bakehouses, and toolsheds. At the other end of the village there was a new church and next to it the only stone house. All the other buildings had half-timbering or were entirely of wood.

The biggest farms had the biggest dung heaps. That seemed logical. A lot of oxen, cows, and horses made more manure than a few geese. And so it was easy to discover who the rich people were.

There were meadows with fruit trees and a few cultivated fields surrounding the village. Beyond the fields was only forest—forest as far as you could see. I wondered where the girl with the braid down to her behind might live.

I walked down the street and back three times. But I never caught sight of the long braid and the girl it belonged to.

Behind the church a track led to the edge of the forest. There appeared to be a small brook and a little lake too. It was beautiful here. You could certainly swim in the lake in summer.

All of a sudden there was a long beanpole of a fellow standing in front of me. I already knew him. It was impossible to overlook him. He sat in the last row. He'd already pulled my hair once this morning, and for no reason at all.

At first he didn't recognize me. Then he laughed like a

madman, and thumped his chest with his fist. "Hey!" he said, showing his gigantic tusks of teeth.

"Hey!" I replied, for it's usually a mistake to pass a strong man without a polite word. But sometimes it's also a mistake to say anything to such people. Like now, for instance. He had his arms thrust into his pants pockets up to the elbows. The great and powerful do that. It raises their prestige.

"Hey!" said the long beanpole. He probably only knew the one word. Again he thumped his fist on his chest, and he kept coming closer. Slowly he tramped up to me.

Then I got scared. I turned fast and ran, which is all I could think to do. I didn't trust this fellow; if he got hold of me, I'd be done for. I was very fast since I didn't have much weight to carry, but Beanpole had legs that were twice as long as mine, and he was gaining on me. I leaned so far forward that I was almost horizontal. He was right behind me. He mustn't catch me. Who knew what he would do to me? Fear spurred me on.

I was almost at the church. He'd probably leave me alone in the village.

Beanpole was just about to grab me, but he didn't. I didn't hear his panting anymore. Had he given up? Yes, he'd given up, just when he was about to catch me. Unbelievable!

Then I saw the reason. There was a boy standing opposite Beanpole. I hadn't seen him during the chase.

It was Christian Knapp. He had his arms cocked as if he was getting ready to fight. He stood there bravely in front of the big fellow. And then something quite remarkable happened. Beanpole turned around and went back to the track.

The Knapp boy was pulling an empty little wagon. Was he going to steal something?

He came up to me.

"Thanks!" I said.

"That's all right!" After a moment he cautioned, "Watch out for Hornigel! He's unpredictable. If you aren't stronger than he is, he'll knock you around."

"Why would he do that?" I asked. "I hardly know him."

"Why? He doesn't know himself." Christian Knapp smiled. "Now I recognize you. You're the new one. My, they sure gave you a trim!" His serious face softened. Two little dimples formed in his cheeks, his eyes crinkled up, and then he laughed. Christian could laugh heartily. Much too pleasant for a robber's son.

"At least you're not a girl anymore. But I liked you better before."

An oxcart went rattling by the church. I was ashamed of myself. Did I really look so stupid that all the world had to laugh at me? It made me angry.

"I have to go to the other end of the village," said Christian. We walked along together.

Funny, two boys in the same class at school, and they trotted along like oxen, not saying anything. That seemed dumb to me. Therefore I asked after a while, "Does the schoolmaster always hit you so hard?"

"What's it to you?" he replied.

Again after a while: "Is it true that your father is a robber?" But I already regretted that I'd asked something so stupid. "Excuse me! That just slipped out of me."

"It doesn't matter!" said Christian. "People say it, and perhaps my father *is* a robber. What else is he supposed to do if all the world is after him?"

Christian Knapp increased his speed. The wagon bounced over the village street. He was in a big hurry, as if he himself were a robber and I wasn't a schoolmate but the police. We reached the middle of the village. The conversation hadn't gone beyond the few sentences.

I was angry with myself. I liked Christian Knapp, and I would have liked to talk with him. But the many questions that I had wouldn't come out. They stayed stuck up there in my head. Devil take it, anyhow! Christian could say something too! He did actually look as if he was going to talk any minute, but nothing came of it.

We went along like two people who were meeting for the first time but already knew each other for goodness knows how long.

Soon we were in the lower village. Christian Knapp said suddenly, "Oh-oh, you're going to get into trouble!"

"Why should I get into trouble?"

"Didn't you see the mayor in the window of the office?"

"Yes, and . . . ?"

"If he saw us, and he *did* see us, then he'll tan your bottom this evening. At least he'll give you a chewing out. Your uncle will lecture you: 'The Knapp boy isn't a fit companion for you, and I don't want to see you with him again!' That's what the mayor will say. Guaranteed."

"Not a Fit Companion!"

AT SUPPER I WAS SITTING between Uncle and Frederika. Uncle wanted it that way.

Thank heavens I had Frederika next to me. It was reassuring.

There was milk soup, and the mayor's folk spooned it up very politely. Only old Daniel smacked his lips a little as he ate. I took the greatest pains to satisfy my hunger slowly and politely.

Uncle talked with the farmhands and maids about the next day's work. He didn't even look at me. What was bothering him?

Then suddenly, in the middle of his discussion with the servants, he turned to me and spoke, not very loudly but not very softly either. "Boniface Schroll!" he said, and the *Schroll* thundered from his mouth quite sternly. "I want to say one thing to you, and mark it well, for I never say things twice. The Knapp boy isn't a fit companion for you. I don't want to see you with him again!" Then he ladled some more milk soup into his plate, broke some bread into it, and asked Daniel why the wild pear tree in the pigpen hadn't been cut down.

I was badly shaken. I didn't know why Uncle had spoken so sternly and venomously, and I was surprised that what he said agreed almost word for word with Christian Knapp's prediction.

I wanted to cry. But I wasn't supposed to do that now that I was a shorn village boy.

Uncle was unfair. How could Knapp help it if he was a robber's son? Was he so dangerous and bad that he had to be treated like a leper?

I swallowed hard and succeeded in suppressing my tears. I wasn't going to cry in front of Uncle. He certainly wouldn't understand that a boy can and must cry. I wanted to become hard like Christian Knapp. He could stand a huge whipping without shedding a single tear!

I said that I was dog tired and had to get some sleep. Frederika looked at me strangely, as if she knew that my tears were secretly tormenting me.

I went straight to my attic.

Uncle had a big house. Certainly it was the biggest in the village. Not even the minister's house could compare with it. Except for Uncle and his servants, no one else lived here. The ground floor smelled of cows and cooking, of old paper, of ink, and of floor sand. The mayor's office and the records room had an office smell.

Right next to Uncle's office was the toilet. It also had a powerful smell. In Cannstatt there was usually paper in the toilet. After Aunt Wilhelmine read the newspaper, she cut it into little sheets. You had to be careful with it. One little sheet, which was exactly one eighth of a newspaper page, had to do for one wipe of your rear end. Uncle, of course, had a newspaper too. But it was the official gazette, with all the royal rules and regulations. Therefore it couldn't be used for wiping behinds. It belonged in the mayor's office, and it was urgently needed there. Instead, you had to use a handful of hay, if you had brought it with you, or your fingers. There was a bucket of water there for washing up. Uncle wouldn't tolerate having the wall smeared.

The small farmers and the day workers didn't have a toilet in the house. They used a pail or they went straight to the dung heap.

Uncle's house was large, but I finally reached my own room up under the roof. I was too tired to think any longer. Even my troubles with Uncle faded. Traces of the most important experiences of the day lingered as part of my dozing dreams: the village, my uncle as God-father, and School-master Altmayer. He remained the longest, and I saw him thrashing stacks of pupils with an extra-long stick. I was wedged between Carl Weber two and Beanpole, who was baring his vicious tusks at me. The girl with the long braid sobbed softly and smiled at me at the same time. Christian Knapp, the robber's son, walked through the village pulling a wagon. He didn't look like a robber's brat, and he was almost as nice-looking as the girl with the braid down to her behind.

Cleanliness Inspection

"GET UP, LAZYBONES! Get up!"

Where was I?

I was startled out of sleep. Well, God be thanked I wasn't in the forest, and I wasn't in bed at Aunt Wilhelmine's in Cannstatt but in my room at Uncle's in Graab.

It was a new day.

There was Frederika standing by the bed, and that was reassuring. The maid looked for my head in the bedclothes. She gave me something like a box on the ear, or maybe it was more like a gentle stroke. Loudly and brassily she cried, "Get up! You have to go to school!"

I closed my eyes again and the maid whisked off the monster featherbed. The fresh March morning air blew through the cracks between the roofboards.

"Out of bed, you sleepyhead!" Frederika scolded, looking

at me utterly dumbfounded. "Do people in the city sleep with nothing on?"

"I don't know. I always sleep naked. My Aunt Wilhelmine said it isn't good to wear your shirt day and night."

I jumped out of bed. It was noticeably cold without goose feathers.

"And you must wash, too!"

I looked for a wash basin but didn't find one. The maid noticed. "There's a pump trough in the yard," she said. "And when the water isn't frozen, the men wash there."

I climbed into my pants and ran downstairs. The stone flags on the ground floor were icy cold. The pump was in the middle of the courtyard. One of the farm maids worked the pump handle, and a powerful stream poured out of the wooden pipe into the bucket.

The maid shook her head. "What a cuckoo!" she scolded. "This crazy city boy has come to wash without his shirt!"

I stuck my hand in the trough. Oh, dear! Good and cold! It was a wonder that this water was still water. It really ought to have been ice.

A small boy from the house next door washed very simply. He splashed a hand full of water over his mouth, nose, and eyes. Done!

I was going to do the same thing. I didn't want too much contact with this icy fluid from the underworld. Perhaps this was the way people in Graab washed. But I didn't even get to finish my thought.

Uncle was standing next to me. He took a pail and filled it, then bent my naked torso over the pump trough and poured the water over me.

A person could die from this! The wet cold iced my skin.

Frederika rushed up. "Mayor!" she cried. "Do you want to kill my boy?" Quickly and vigorously she rubbed me dry with her coarse linen apron.

A nice feeling of well-being prickled under my skin. I liked Frederika. Sometime I must tell her.

Then, almost in passing, Uncle gibed, "You see! It wasn't half so bad, and if you do it every morning, you'll quickly get used to it!"

What a monster! I thought. But at least he had bothered with me. So I meant something to my uncle.

"You have to get to school, boy!" Frederika urged. "But you should eat something first, so hurry up!"

I dashed up the stairs, hurried into my shirt, shoes, stockings, and jacket, then ran down to the kitchen, quickly ate a slice of bread, and gulped down a glass of milk still warm from the cow.

Frederika was wonderful! If she hadn't had such a brassy voice she could have become my second mother.

The young farmhand came into the kitchen. He looked around curiously, and when he noticed that I had gotten bread with honey on it, his face filled with envy.

"Don't look so jealous!" Frederika reproved him. "I just have to fatten up this starving Boniface. You're fat enough!" She ran both hands over my shorn stubble, pressed a few flattened hairs upright, and sighed. "Now, get going this minute!" she said in her brassy voice. "There are no more little children on the street, and the clock's just about to strike eleven. The schoolmaster will give you trouble if you're late."

Oh, not that! I remembered the long, supple stick and the whistling blows.

What time was it in Cannstatt now? I had to get used to the three-hour conversion.

The upper class was already full, and the air was already unbreathable again. The lesson hadn't begun yet. It wasn't warm and it wasn't cold—rather, it was uncomfortably in-between. The room was no longer heated. Why? Because it was March? Was it *ever* heated? It probably wasn't necessary. The children themselves heated it so well that any stove would have been too much by the second hour.

With effort I squeezed in next to Carl Weber two. Up front, in the second row of girls, I saw the beautiful long braid. Way back in the last row of boys crouched Beanpole. He stared at me venomously. Why did he hate me so? I hadn't done anything to him. Christian Knapp sat diagonally in front of him. Thank God he was there. I smiled at him. He again got those pleasant dimples in his cheeks and smiled back.

The door flew open. Herr Schoolmaster Altmayer went directly to a desk in front of the blackboard, took the stick in his hand, and banged it on the desk.

"Quiet!"

It was immediately silent in the upper class. No one wanted to attract attention, for that would mean trouble. A prayer was said in unison.

I was eager to take part in the lesson. Perhaps today I could show what kind of Latin scholar I was. I wanted them to see that I also knew something.

But the lesson didn't begin yet. Plainly faking ignorance, the schoolmaster asked after "the new girl-boy, a certain Boniface Schroll, who had arrived yesterday." He couldn't see him anywhere. "Please, where is he, then?" And he grimaced.

"Here's Schroll!" the class whinnied, and Carl Weber two ran his hand over my stubble, taking obvious pleasure in my discomfort.

I was paralyzed. I clenched my fists. It would have been good if I could have died, and fast! This shameful humiliation!

Didn't the schoolmaster see my anger? Wasn't he afraid I'd tell my uncle?

Time was passing, but still no proper lesson. Cleanliness inspection!

"Gottlieb Bay! Display your handkerchief!"

Gottlieb Bay pulled a small linen cloth out of his trouser pocket and held it up. Everyone could see that it was for show only.

"Very well! All right, then. Everyone!"

Now all the boys and girls fished into their trouser and apron pockets. A great variety of cloths were produced. Obviously, all of them were show handkerchiefs.

What kind of nonsense was this, I wondered. Why did the schoolmaster let them show handkerchiefs they never used?

It was plainly fraud! The teacher *wanted* to be tricked! What a circus!

The schoolmaster looked here, looked there, and then nodded. Perhaps he was satisfied with the inspection, or perhaps it was too much trouble for him to look carefully. "Put them away!" he commanded.

Pause.

"Friedrich Fuenfkorn! Your hands!"

The one named lifted his hands over his head so the teacher could examine them.

"Filth!" snarled the schoolmaster. "Come here, you pig!"

Friedrich Fuenfkorn clattered forward, received two sturdy blows on his palms, and made his way back to his seat with a tearful face.

Long pause. There was something in the air. The entire upper class felt it. Herr Schoolmaster thought for a long time. He savored the anxiety of the boys and girls.

I made myself very small, hoping I wouldn't be the next one he picked on.

The pause grew longer. Everyone was breathing with great care, and all eyes were fixed on our desks. Just don't notice me!

"Knapp!" screamed the schoolmaster. "Come here!"

A sigh in the upper class. Thank God, it was only Knapp.

The victim crept forward over pupils and desks. His face was very pale. I knew, and the class knew, and Christian Knapp of course knew, too, that the schoolmaster was now going to make mincemeat out of him. The son of a robber has to bear everything. He must be held up as a terrible example.

"Knapp, take your shoes off!"

The boy grew even paler. Somewhere in my heart arose a mighty, un-Christian rage. That was mean! Did you even have to show your feet?

The schoolmaster wanted to humiliate Knapp. Of course, only him!

"Well, is it going to be soon, robber boy?"

Knapp slipped out of his shoes. His anxious eyes were ablaze with hatred. I was both hot and cold. Why did I have so much compassion for the robber's son? I wanted to convince myself that it didn't matter to me if Knapp was humiliated and beaten. But it did. I wished the plague on the schoolmaster and I crossed my fingers for Christian Knapp. Someone in the second row of girls was crying again.

Students in the back rows stood on their desks so as not to miss anything. Strange! The schoolmaster allowed it.

Astonishment! No one had expected this: There were no holes in his stockings, no toes sticking out, and the stockings were clean.

Looking at the schoolmaster, you could see that he was disappointed. He'd expected something else. "Take them off!" he commanded. "Take the stockings off!"

Knapp pulled off his stockings. His feet were tanned but clean. The toenails had no black borders.

"Oh!" gasped the children in front in a chorus, and most were certainly thinking of their own not-so-clean feet.

"Quiet!" hissed the schoolmaster, banging his stick on the desk. "You are a pig. You robber brat!"

The schoolmaster hesitated for a long time.

"Your feet are dirty!"

All the blood left Christian Knapp's face. The boy looked dead. A mountain of rage boiled in me. But I didn't let it show because I was terrified of the schoolmaster. I only stared at a hole in the desk and focused my anger and loathing there.

Finally the lesson began.

But even then I had no chance to show off my Latin. An hour of arithmetic. In the foreordained order the times tables were recited, and it was astonishing how well everyone knew the counting rhymes.

I noticed the voice of the girl with the braid down to her behind. It was anxious and trembling.

Second hour. Stories of the apostles and the geography of Palestine. The schoolmaster hung a map of the Holy Land on the board. He pointed to the blue spots with his stick, and the upper class said in unison: the Mediterranean Sea, the Dead Sea, the Sea of Galilee. The brown spots: the Arabian Desert and the mountains of Judea. The little circles: Jericho, Capernaum, and Emmaus. Then he pointed to where Sodom and Gomorrah once stood, before God destroyed them root and branch in righteous anger. The girls in the front row pointed out Jerusalem and Bethlehem.

Third hour. Recitation. The pious sayings ran through the rows of pupils without any mistakes. They were about the gentleness and severity of the Lord. I could understand some of them, but most had so many unfamiliar words that their meaning remained hidden. I ought to ask the schoolmaster about them. He could surely explain what this or that saying

meant. Just in time I remembered Uncle's pronouncement:
Pupils have to answer. Only the teacher asks questions.

Then it was noon.

I hurried. Perhaps I could see the girl with the braid down to
her behind up close? I pushed myself to the front. But I didn't
make it. The braid had already disappeared through the door.

The Gendarme's Report

SOON AFTER THAT the Devil himself was loosed in the village.

The church tower clock struck quarter past three. We were just sitting down to the noonday meal around the big table. Uncle lifted his spoon and dipped it into the barley soup. That was the sign for the others to begin eating. And they did so at varying speeds, though the young farmhand was without doubt the fastest. I myself had developed a powerful hunger during the course of the morning, and so I jumped right in.

Just at that moment the gendarme entered the house.

He came straight into the kitchen. Apparently he knew exactly where the mayor would be. He saluted. "Gendarme Grimmerlich here to report!"

"What do you want, now, just at midday?" asked the mayor.

"Permission to report, sir. Urgent!"

"Then report, Grimmerlich! But quickly, before the soup gets cold."

"Permission to report, sir. It's strictly official business!" As he spoke he looked at me and the servants. "It is strictly official!" he repeated.

Somewhat annoyed, the mayor laid down his spoon, stood up, and led the way into the office next door.

I saw the annoyance on Uncle's face.

"Now, then, report!" I heard. Then the door closed.

All we could hear from the mayor's office was an indecipherable murmur. Even listening through the keyhole did no good, but the curious young farmhand tried, first with one ear, then the other. No one except the mayor heard what the gendarme had to report.

"The gendarme is stationed over in Laemmersbach because he's needed there more than here with us," old Daniel explained to me. "He has an hour and a half's journey to us," he added. "So he comes only when he's called, or if there's some criminal action over on his side."

Frederika observed that it must be an extraordinary crime if the gendarme came himself and the matter could keep the mayor from his noon meal for so long.

"The gendarme always has a gun with him," old Daniel told me. "The gun makes him a person to be respected. Without the gun he'd be like a naked preacher."

Suddenly the door flew open, and the mayor stood in the doorway. The young hand tried to jump away.

"Stop! Stay here! Run straight to Police Constable Fuenf-korn and order him to report to me at once. At once, I said!"

The door closed again, and still not one person knew what all this noonday secrecy was about. It had to be something bad!

A few minutes passed, then Beadle and Police Constable Fuenfkorn, tripping twice and sweaty-faced, entered the kitchen. He only needed to knock on the mayor's office door once, and it opened immediately. Saluting, he disappeared into the room.

Somewhat later we heard the loud, inimitable voice of the police constable. It didn't just penetrate doors and windows like a normal one but even came through thick walls. Still, we could not make out what he was saying. The police constable trumpeted only one word throughout the house, and this one word, *"Exakt,"* was familiar to everyone in the village. Fuenfkorn used it a hundred times a day.

The discussion came to an end after half an hour. The gendarme and the constable came out of the village office. Their faces were official and uncommunicative.

However, before the gendarme set out on his homeward walk to Laemmersbach, he fortified himself at the Stag. And because the constable was also severely stressed, he went with him. The beer was good, and the Stag's barkeeper kept refilling the glasses. He was curious, and a few beers didn't mean anything to him.

After the fourth glass the secret was out. Constable Fuenf-korn was the first to let it slip. The under maid, who was taking eggs to the preacher, overheard the news and immediately ran back to the mayor's house.

Robber Knapp had attacked the under ox drover from Huetten two nights before. He had ambushed him in the forest between Boehringsweiler and Wuestenroth and jumped him from behind with a knife. The robber had bagged 300 gulden. That was a huge fortune, enough for the villain to live in the lap of luxury for five years or more. The under ox drover was also injured during the attack. It was plain to see. Naturally not the wound itself, of course, but a thick bandage on his upper arm.

No doubt about it, the robber was none other than Knapp. The under ox drover could describe him from head to toe.

But I had thought that it was Robber Knapp who found me in the forest and carried me into the village. Maybe I'd only dreamed of the big black hat, but I thought I saw it. Knapp never went without that hat. But now I had to believe he couldn't have been the one. For at almost the same time he was attacking the under ox drover somewhere else entirely. Even a topnotch robber can't be in two places far away from each other at the same time.

Poor Christian. This would be a bad day for you. Why didn't you choose another father? That was all nonsense, of course, for no one can choose his father. Not even Christian Knapp.

The Stranger

THE DAYS CAME and went. I'd been in Graab for a week and a half now. I knew many villagers, and they all knew me. The mayor's house was always buzzing with people coming and going. Actually, the people who were around the most were the rich horse farmers, who were always involved when there were things to be decided. They made up the village council, the citizens' committee, the church board of trustees, the church convention, the local school board, and the welfare agency. They helped the mayor and the minister govern the village, as much the king would allow.

Was that right? But who else would have cared about the village? The small ox or cow farmers? Or the utterly poor geese keepers? They always had enough to do taking care of themselves and their poverty. How could they concern themselves about the community and the needs of other people too?

In a village there are all kinds of people, and some are gossips. They are terribly clever, and they always know exactly what other people should do or shouldn't do. One day I overheard the schoolmaster's wife and the preacher's wife gossiping about me. I noticed because they were staring at me so maliciously. "He even laughs, the orphan boy," the schoolmaster's wife carped. "He probably doesn't even know that being an orphan is a sad lot."

Sunday had turned out to be magnificently beautiful. In the early morning, a warm spring rain sprinkled the region, and anyone with proper eyes in his head could see how impatiently the grass, leaves, and the first flowers were growing.

Right after the rain the sun rose in the heavens, and the day managed to show God's creation in an absolutely beautiful light. Thank God for Sundays! Not only because of the meals, but because for me it was a day without the schoolmaster.

The farmers, the hands, and the maids got up with the roosters even on Sundays. There was work to do as on any other day. The cattle still had to eat and be milked, and they didn't make any less manure just because it was Sunday. But there was no field work on Sundays, not even wood chopping, and no butchering. Nothing except for things that absolutely must be done and could not be put off.

After the morning barn work the people washed their faces and hands, put on their Sunday clothes, and went to Church. Everyone! Kith and kin! Only a few old and sick people who didn't really know if they were alive or dead and so couldn't or wouldn't move didn't have to go to church. Otherwise, the church fathers saw to it that no one stayed home without an excuse. They sent the inspector from house to house to enforce the Sunday laws. Anyone caught at home, possibly even still at work, was quickly made poorer by a few gulden. Those who wouldn't or couldn't pay went to the village jail. The other villagers could then view the godless one through the jail window for a few days afterward. Of course all of Graab was in church on this particular Sunday. Who ever had any extra gulden? Or who wanted to be exhibited in the jail like a heathen or a prize ox or a deformed calf?

People were just coming out of church. A few men were still standing together, the others having gone next door to the Pony. The women and maids were hurrying home so that Sunday dinner would be on the table in time.

Then a strange man came into the village.

No one knew him. Even old Shoemaker Gottlieb Fritzen had never seen him before, and there was no one in the entire back forest unknown to him.

Who was this stranger? Where did he come from? What was he doing here? He didn't look ragged or ill-fed, so he wasn't a beggar. He didn't have a tray on his front or a pack on his back, so he couldn't be a peddler.

All eyes followed him mistrustfully. Village Councilor Raber was the first to say what everyone was thinking. "This stranger can't be an honest man. Respectable travelers never go on foot. They travel in a chaise or a coach. Maybe he's one of those newfangled atheists. Otherwise he'd be in church in his village or in his city now. In any case, he must be up to no good. He should move on before he makes any trouble."

The strange man stopped in front of the church.

"Good morning!" he said to the men standing there together.

No one answered him, because no one trusted him.

"A blessedly beautiful day today," said the stranger. "A perfect day for walking in glorious nature."

I was surprised that no one wanted to talk with this friendly, cheerful man. The stranger probably thought it was quite odd that no one answered him. The church folk continued to eye him mistrustfully, like a thief. Some sort of miscreant he definitely was, and in any case he was a Sabbath-breaker. Any man who went walking into strange places on Sunday without a reason must certainly have a heap of skeletons in his closet. Such people had no business in Graab.

Then this man, still standing in front of the church, sang a song. It was extraordinarily beautiful. No one in the entire village could sing so beautifully, and all the men and children standing in front of the church listened to him. I thought they enjoyed it. Anyone who could sing that well couldn't be a bad man, even if he was a stranger.

The schoolmaster hurried by, faster and faster. He hurried down to the lower village. He was certainly up to something!

Shortly thereafter Police Constable Fuenfkorn strode up. "Quiet!" he bellowed.

The stranger jumped. He stopped singing.

"*Exakt!*" said Fuenfkorn loudly. He went up to him. "It is

the charge of the schoolmaster here—and if he doesn't know, who does?—that such a thing is not permitted. A worldly song, in which God is not mentioned even once, may not be sung in public on Sunday, and most certainly not on the street right in front of the church. It isn't right, no matter how beautiful the song is. *Exakt!*" the constable finished. He took the Sabbath-breaker firmly by the arm and led him to the mayor's house. There he locked him up in the local jail.

Now he was sitting there, locked away from the glorious spring Sunday.

I was both furious and sad. I'd seen and heard it all, and I couldn't find the slightest fault with the stranger. On the contrary, he was merely happy and cheerful, and he hadn't intended anything but to give pleasure. I wanted to tell the man that he could sing wonderfully. Someone should do it! I walked around the jail twice. Then I took a pail that was standing in front of the barn, turned it over, climbed up on it, and looked through the little window.

There the stranger with the beautiful voice was sitting, motionless, on a wooden bed with a straw mattress. I couldn't see his face, but he was looking at the door, as if he expected someone to come and take him out of this dark hole.

The day wasn't beautiful anymore, even if the sun was making such an effort. Now I hated the village.

Frederika was working in the kitchen. She was just cutting spaetzle.

"Is something the matter, boy?"

"No, not really. Tell me, Frederika, where's my uncle?"

"He's at the minister's house. The church convention is meeting. And then he plans to visit the Sunday School."

"Fuenfkorn has locked up a stranger!"

"Yes, I know."

"But he didn't do anything. He only sang a wonderful song very beautifully."

"He's not allowed to do that on Sunday."

"But why not? And must he be locked up for it?"

"Yes. Until the mayor has determined the fine."

"A fine? And if the stranger can't pay?"

"Then he'll stay locked up for some time. And besides, the offense has to be reported to his home parish."

"Is Fuenfkorn the only one with a key to the jail?"

"The mayor has one too, of course. It's in the desk drawer in his office. But why are you asking such useless stuff?"

"Just asking."

Why was Frederika looking at me so oddly? Had she noticed something?

I sneaked around the jail again and pondered. The stranger was certainly in jail unfairly. He hadn't done anything wrong. Singing couldn't be bad. Certainly Fuenfkorn had made a mistake in his zeal for duty. Something had to be done, and I knew exactly what it was.

Quickly I ran to the top end of the village and once around the schoolhouse. It was unusually quiet. The mayor must be there already.

All the young people had to go to Sunday School after they had finished with the village school. For three years they had to sit there, Sunday after Sunday, on the narrow school benches. But the half-grown farmers' sons and farmhands were too big to be intimidated by the schoolmaster's rod anymore. Who, after all, would try to punish the treelike Adam Jaeggle with the stick? He could lift Altmayer with one hand and smash him on the floor if he wanted to. It took the threat of steep fines to force the Sunday School pupils to the school bench.

Everyone was afraid of the mayor. He wasn't only a strong man, he was also an official who deserved respect. Anyone who threatened the mayor had to reckon with the worst, because he was lifting his hand against the king, as it were. The mayor was, in fact, the arm of the king in the village.

If it was so quiet in the Sunday School, the mayor was surely there. I ran back to the mayor's house again. My uncle would certainly not be home for another half hour. That was enough time.

I went into the kitchen and considered how I could get the key to the jail.

"Do you want something?" Frederika asked. "Are you looking for something, boy?"

"No," I lied.

"Then sit down here and tell me about the world or about the railroad in Cannstatt. Is it true that you've ridden on it?" Frederika was looking at me strangely, as if she knew exactly what I was thinking.

I didn't really have my mind on it, but I had to tell her something. Otherwise she'd be suspicious. Every now and then I would steal a look at the office door. It was never closed. Behind it was the desk with the drawer, and in it lay the key to the jail.

Perhaps Frederika would go to the cellar, or need eggs from the chicken house. She might have to go to the bathroom.

I sat and told her something or other about how I had taken the train to Untertuerkheim. I hoped Frederika didn't notice how nervous I was. There was still nobody else at home, but soon the mayor and the young farmhand would be back from Sunday School. Old Daniel had gone into the Stag right after church. He was well out of the way there, though he would certainly be home punctually for dinner.

Frederika looked at me oddly.

"Hey, Boniface," she said suddenly. "I just remembered that the boot grease is all gone. Quick, run down to Merchant Heldmaier and bring me a lump of the new black. You don't need any money. He'll put it on the tab. Now, get going! If Heldmaier is just sitting down to eat, he won't open up for you again."

Devil take it, I growled to myself. It was like black magic! I wasn't going to be able to get the key. Probably nothing would come of my plan.

"Boot grease, today, on Sunday?" I asked.

"The storekeeper does his best business on Sunday. All the people come to church, and then they go shopping at his store."

At the store Fuenfkorn's wife and the Widow Schick were

gossiping away. I had to wait quite a while, because Merchant Heldmaier was gossiping with them.

Fuenfkorn's wife wanted tooth cotton.

"This is really outstanding!" said the grocer. "It stops any sort of toothache immediately. I just got it in last week. A paperful only costs nine kreuzer. Very highly recommended!"

I waited. Would I ever get my boot grease?

Fuenfkorn's wife wanted a small bottle of ice pomade and a cake of tar soap. She would only have tar soap, since she had the best experience with it. There was not a single blemish on her skin.

"What don't they have nowadays!" said the Widow Schick. She probably didn't have any soap at all at home.

The wife of rich farmer Raber came into the shop. She wanted some salt in a hurry. She had run out yesterday, and you can't be without salt in the kitchen. Heldmaier served her at once. Frau Raber was so rich that he couldn't keep her waiting.

I waited for my boot grease.

The grocer praised a new kind of beard-growing tincture. Naturally not for the ladies, but perhaps for their sons or grandsons. A guaranteed product that by itself would produce the strongest beard growth in even very young people in the shortest time.

I asked boldly if I could not have a lump of boot grease.

The four looked at me, flabbergasted. Frau Fuenfkorn said cattily, "Don't young people today have any manners or respect for their elders?"

Then the grocer, Fuenfkorn, Raber, and the Widow Schick nattered on about the efficacy of gout pads and every other possible novelty. I finally got my boot grease, and I hurried home. Too late! My uncle was already there.

"What do you want with boot grease?" he asked me.

"I? Nothing! Frederika needed it!"

"Why does the woman need boot grease again? She just bought a lump two weeks ago!"

Then it was finally dinnertime. The noonday table was already occupied. The young hand looked at Frederika with hungry eyes. When would she bring in the pots and pans?

Instead, Fuenfkorn arrived. He begged to report, sir, that after church he had arrested a Sabbath-breaker and imprisoned him. This strange man had not only stood in front of the church on the holy Sabbath for no good reason—that is correct, only *in front of*. No, he had not gone into the church. And he even sang a song in the churchyard, and this song was not from the hymn book, and in this song God was not mentioned one single time.

The mayor wanted to eat and was annoyed. "Bring him right in! He shall pay one gulden. Then he can go on his way."

Fuenfkorn's typically red face was cheesy white when he came back to the kitchen after a while. He came in alone, without the prisoner.

"Where's the delinquent?" asked the mayor.

The constable swallowed, then stammered so badly that hardly anyone could understand him. "Don't know . . . devilry! The godless man isn't there anymore . . . he's missing. The jail is empty."

"Fuenfkorn!" chided the mayor. "You locked him up yourself. So he ought to be in there."

"He ought to be! But he isn't! Witchcraft! I don't know what's going on!"

"Don't talk nonsense. You probably didn't lock the jail door. The stranger can hardly have passed through the walls, and the little window is much too small. Fuenfkorn! Fuenfkorn," hissed the mayor angrily. "You're really not much good anymore!"

The beadle and police constable left the kitchen crestfallen. He saluted all the way into the yard. He kept peering into the jail, as if what should not be could not be. How was it that the godless one wasn't there anymore?

No one in the mayor's house, however, was at all gloomy during the midday meal. Frederika seemed to be in a particularly good mood.

I also had a light heart. The injustice to the stranger had been resolved on its own. God brings order to everything at the proper time. You can usually rely on that.

But what was the matter with Frederika? Her face seemed to be smiling of its own accord—shyly, perhaps, but visible to anyone.

She winked at me. What a thing! I hope she didn't see that I blushed because she winked at me. Tomorrow I would certainly tell her that I liked her.

CLever Frederika

DURING DINNER, Uncle said that I should take a leisurely little look around the district. Not too far, and I shouldn't get myself lost again. So that afternoon I decided to walk around the village.

The day was still beautiful. It was a little like summer. The birds were back again, and they appeared, without exception, to be in good humor. They twittered and whistled and crowed and trilled and sang. They did it so rapturously and loudly that I didn't hear anything else.

I climbed up the slope, there, where deep in the forest the high field must be. Before I went into the forest, I looked all around. Down below in the meadowlands lay the village of Graab. It sparkled, from inn yard to cemetery. The farther away I went, the more beautiful it became! The distance polished away the dirty spots, and from so far away, the many dung heaps and liquid-manure ditches didn't smell, either.

The road climbed up the mountain, into the middle of the forest.

I recalled the terrible night I had had a week and a half before. But by day the forest wasn't mysterious at all. The sun shone down into it and made it friendly. Today especially. Would I be able to find the place where I had gotten lost?

I felt like an explorer. A giant, unfamiliar primeval forest lay before me. Far below, in a deep gorge, there was water rushing. That could have been where the man in the black hat found me and brought me to the village. Funny, no one wanted to admit that he had saved me. It had to have been somebody, and certainly this somebody was from this place. No stranger would walk or drive through these forests at night, nor would he have been able to move about without being seen or heard. Besides, who would be going around in the forest at night? Only poachers and robbers!

That was a gruesome night. I got goose pimples on my back just thinking about it. I kept hiking upward until I came to a crossroads. It could have been here that I went in the wrong direction. In fact, there *was* something like a wagon track going down steeply.

The eagerness of an explorer seized me. I pushed aside all reasonable objections and decided to climb down through the forest toward where I heard the water rushing. I wasn't afraid. As long as it was day I would certainly find the road again. I only needed to climb back up on the same path. Then I would get back on the road. Simple.

I jumped over ditches and brooklets and clambered over

fallen tree trunks. All at once the sun was gone. It never penetrated way down here. Larger and smaller streams and brooks fell into the ravine from all sides. The last remnants of snow had turned to water with the morning's rain. It burbled and splashed and gurgled and rushed. Where all the many streams came together the frothing and tumbling stopped. Almost soundlessly the brook, now broad, pushed its way through the valley.

Down here by the water stood gigantic trees. They stretched so high that they too got a piece of heaven and a few beams of sun. One of the trunks was so big that it would have taken three or four boys to ring that colossus.

A giant fallen tree blocked the ravine. I wanted to crawl under it, but there was no managing it. So I balanced on this tree bridge, pushing through massive branches, over the water. I sat on the mighty trunk and stretched out. My back tingled pleasantly when I let my legs dangle over the water. The danger underneath was delightfully creepy. I felt as if I were riding a ship through the forest.

On the slope a roe deer dashed past.

Down below, at the bend, I saw two forms moving. They were visible for only a very brief moment. They were also climbing on a trunk lying crosswise. Then they were gone.

I felt a rush of fear. The large figure had on a black hat. Could it be Robber Knapp? Perhaps! Perhaps not, too! People said he always wore a big black hat.

I hurried up the slope. Even if it wasn't Knapp down there, safer is surer! Just get away from here in a hurry. Back on the road. Nothing much could happen to me in broad daylight. I didn't want to meet up with the robber in the ravine. Nobody would search for me or find me down there if the robber did me in.

Soon I was in the sunny part of the forest again. I looked around a few times, but there was no one behind me. I saw and heard nothing suspicious. Only the birds chattering on and on, and the rivulets of water splashing into the narrow defile down below. A path or an animal track led slantwise to the slope to the top, past carpets of wood anemones.

Then I was on the road again. Slowly I sauntered back toward the village. At the edge of the forest I sat down on a tree stump. The afternoon sun warmed my back.

I sat there for a while. Something uneven was sticking into my right buttock. I was just looking for a more comfortable position when he walked past. Christian Knapp, the son of the robber. He was looking along the edge of the forest, down to the village, up the road, and down into the forest. Then he went on. He didn't see me. I was sitting quietly on the stump, and my green Sunday jacket blended so well with the forest that I looked like growing greenery.

If I'd still had any doubts, now I knew for certain. It was Robber Knapp I saw before down in the ravine, and the second figure was no one other than Christian, his son.

Perhaps the robber's hiding place was right down there. Uncle would certainly be very glad if he knew the villain's hiding place. I thought it over. Should I or shouldn't I?

No, I wouldn't do it! No one would believe me anyway— me, the coward from the city who had just been in Graab for a week and a half and was already smarter than the entire village and the authorities. I was also afraid of the robber. What would a robber do to a half-pint like me if he found out that I had squealed on him?

God protect me from that!

Therefore I'd just keep my secret to myself!

Until that night.

Sleep would not come, although I was terribly tired. My conscience bothered me and my head throbbed. I couldn't cope with it. It gave me no peace. Robber Knapp was a criminal, my conscience told me, and a criminal belonged in prison. If I knew where his hideout was, then I had to report it to the authorities. Otherwise, my conscience thundered, I was a criminal too.

I resolved to report what I had seen that afternoon. I put my trousers on and went down to the kitchen. Only Frederika was there. She was washing pots and pans.

"Is something the matter, boy?" she asked with concern.

"Yes," I answered. "I have to tell you something important!"

"Now, at night?"

"Yes, it's tormenting me!"

"If that's so, tell me what's so important."

I told her that I'd seen Robber Knapp and that I might perhaps know where his hideout was.

"You don't say!" she marveled. "And are you certain that it was Knapp? Did you recognize him?"

"No."

"How do you know you saw him, then?"

"Afterwards I saw his son, Christian, on the road."

"And did he come from down below, from the brook?"

"I'm not sure."

"Well, then, you see, Boniface? We had better keep our noses out of this, because we can't prove anything. I think now you can sleep in peace."

How clever Frederika was. She was always so reasonable, and she knew just the right thing every time! A person simply had to like her.

Tomorrow I would tell her that I liked her.

The Spring Poem

ONCE IN A BLUE MOON a miracle occurred in Graab.

Today, for instance. Herr Schoolmaster had a good day. That was said to be as rare as a gulden in the almsbox. Something like that only happened once or twice a year, they said. No one knew why Altmayer was normal only one percent of the time and why ninety-nine percent of the time he treated the village children so foully. Today he didn't wallop the desk even once. The rod lay untouched on the ledge of the blackboard. The devil only knew what was going on. Was it spring? For half the morning he talked of the awakening of nature and of the beauty of the season.

We learned a poem.

"Once more spring flutters her blue ribbon through the air."

The rhyme was as smooth as butter and quite catchy. A poet named Mörike had written it.

"No one before him ever described spring so beautifully. One must simply marvel," said the schoolmaster, "that a human being can think that way. This is what makes a poet immortal."

I looked at the girl with the braid down to her behind. She fit so well with spring and the poem. Why were her eyes always red from crying? The girl was very pretty. There was none prettier.

Whenever I saw the long braid, something strange happened. My heart began to thump and my blood ran up to my head and back down again. I hoped no one noticed that I always blushed then. Such an excitable heart! Because of a girl!

After the noonday meal I had to feed the chickens. I watched them. They were diligently picking up each grain. They laid gigantic eggs when they fed so greedily.

I sauntered through the farmyard. The lake meadow ended at the edge of the mayor's farm. Thousands of cowslips were growing in the damp field. They were an egg-yolk yellow, with long stems. A cherry tree was just setting its first pinkish-white flower buds. The branches of the pear trees were also beginning to be dotted with white. The apple branches showed nothing yet except a little green. Now that the snow had melted, the lake was full to its edges. They said it was never so full the rest of the year.

A lark hovered above me. It trilled without stopping and flapped its wings, hovering in the same spot. Perhaps it was hanging from the sky on some invisible thread.

The spring poem had been easy to memorize, and it

remained in my head without any effort. I liked it, and I recited it aloud. Nobody was listening to me there except the mice or sparrows or the lark above me.

At the top of the lake meadow I noticed someone sitting directly under the pear tree.

I ended the poem, hoping whoever it was hadn't heard me. Otherwise he or she might think I had a titmouse or a cricket or a spider in my brain or some other mental illness.

It was Christian Knapp who was under the pear tree. I wasn't supposed to associate with him. My uncle forbade it, and if he saw me, there would be the devil to pay.

Carefully I looked back toward the mayor's place. No one could see me from there. Still, you never knew!

Certainly Knapp had recognized me and probably also heard me. But I didn't care.

He was looking at me. I just went on normally, not looking directly at him.

"Aha!" said Christian, when I was about to pass him. "Your uncle did forbid it! I knew it right off."

"Yes," I said. "What am I going to do? He forbids it!"

I stopped, for I could not just go on as if nothing mattered. That wouldn't be right. And Uncle couldn't see up to the pear tree.

Knapp's eyes were red and wet. A robber's son didn't cry!

Should I ask him if something was wrong? Later perhaps. Not now. And would he want that?

A thrush hopped back and forth between us, pecking to the left, and pecking to the right. I couldn't tell what she was eating—she was so fast.

Christian looked perfectly normal. Even l
other village boys. He had a clean face, almos
Yes! He really did resemble the little one wi
down to her behind.

What the dickens! Did I have to see this gir
braid everywhere?

I stood there in front of Christian. He was sile
said nothing either.

Some time passed. Another thrush looked for wo
something else edible.

I couldn't keep standing there stupidly like an ox. \
would Knapp think of me then?

He smiled at me. Again I saw the little dimples in
cheeks and, ignoring my uncle's commandment, sat dov
silently beside him.

After a while I asked, "Do you know the poem by
heart yet?"

"Yes!"

Behind the orchard meadow a team of oxen headed into
the village. The flock of geese at the weir were protesting so
loudly and excitedly that their cackling carried all the way
up here. I should say something. But nothing that occurred
to me was appropriate. So I began to recite the spring poem.

Christian Knapp held back a little, then he joined in. He
had a good voice, and he put his heart into it. At first we
weren't quite together. But by the time we got to the second
verse, we were as one voice.

"Robber Knapp Is Going to Get It in the Neck!"

LIFE IS SO FULL OF SURPRISES. In the morning the world can seem perfectly ordinary, and then it turns out not be an ordinary day at all.

Like today. By early morning the village was filled with gendarmes from the entire district and everybody who was anybody was there—the village councilors, the citizens' committee, the foresters, of course the beadle and police constable, and many others. What was going on?

"Robber Knapp is going to get it in the neck!"

My uncle was in charge. In the course of the day, Herr Senior Clerk from Backnang also joined them. He intended to put the heavy chains on Knapp with his own hands.

I was torn this way and that. On the one hand, I wanted Uncle to be successful, and on the other hand, I didn't want Christian's father to get caught. That was an unsurmount-

able difficulty. I was for Uncle and I was also for Christian, but somewhat more for Christian.

In the course of the morning the entire troop went into the great forest in search of the robber.

In the early afternoon the first men returned—the old, fat, footsore village councilors. I ran over and questioned them. They had nothing spectacular to report. No, they hadn't caught the robber yet, hadn't even seen him, heard him, or smelled him.

In the evening the final group returned, also without success. Wherever was the rogue hiding? The dogs hadn't discovered the robber either. Except for numbers of abandoned fox and badger burrows, mindless barking, and vain hare chasing, they had found nothing.

Herr Senior Clerk had gone back to Backnang in his chaise long before. He didn't like driving through the forest in the dark. Because of Robber Knapp!

My uncle was the very last one to come home, like a captain who only left his ship just before it sank below the waves.

He was disappointed. "This is like looking for a needle in a haystack!" he said. "Knapp isn't so easy to catch!"

Frederika brought the pot of sour-milk soup. "Perhaps it's better so," she said as an aside.

Old Daniel couldn't conceal his delight over the searchers' ill fortune. It showed on his face. "It's all way overdone!" he said. "No one thinks of cutting up a whole sheet to make a handkerchief; and no one will pull down his house because one stone in the cellar is loose."

Uncle was already looking quite sour. But the chief farm-hand didn't stop. "I've known Knapp since he was boy," he said. "He was never bad, and now everyone blames him for goodness knows what, when he can't defend himself. As every child knows, the tamest ox will become dangerous if he's driven into a corner."

"Enough now!" said Uncle sharply. "That business with the under ox drover went too far! The law must remain the law! The army must be called in. Perhaps we will send for the entire garrison from Ludwigsburg. That's the only way we're going to catch him. We may do just that if Knapp becomes too bold and brazen!"

The schoolmaster arrived. He wanted to talk with Herr Mayor, in private, of course, for he had an idea. About Knapp I was sure.

Both of them went into the office.

"That will be something!" muttered old Daniel. "Nothing good ever comes of it when the schoolmaster thinks."

Daniel didn't like the schoolmaster. That delighted me. I asked him, "Is Knapp as wicked as my uncle says?"

"What do I know? In the old days he was as normal and respectable as I or your uncle. The Knapps owned two pastures, a medium-sized field behind the house, and he had three cows in their barn. Then Knapp had a lot of bad luck. For four or five years. It began with the scarlet fever epidemic. In Graab alone, fifty-three children died in a space of three months. Knapp's little Luise was the first one to get sick, then his six-year-old Wilhelm. Knapp rushed to Murrhardt. There was a good surgeon there. It cost him two cows, and the children died anyway. Then the last cow ate a rusty carpenter's nail in the hay. Nobody knows how the piece of iron got into the cow's feed. But the cow died a horrible death. At first Knapp still had some food in the house. When that was used up, the neighbors helped. Then that ended because there was a famine throughout the country, and the neighbors themselves were chewing their fingers. Knapp had to resort to borrowing money. The interest on the money ate up the pastures first, then the field, and finally the house. Hunger came to the Knapps, and it never left them. Once when the hunger was particularly bad, Knapp stole one of the thirty or forty hens from that rotten Gayer over at Schoenbronn. He tried to pick out the oldest, toughest chicken so that he wouldn't be taking a good layer. But Knapp was a very clumsy thief and was caught immediately. So it began, the criminal career of the Robber Knapp. He sat in the district prison for forty-eight hours because of that old, tough hen. Six months later he trapped a hare in the district of Chief Forester Komerel. Naturally he was caught then, too. Because of the hare he fell into the jurisdiction of the superior judge in Backnang. He was in the lockup for two weeks that time. Knapp almost didn't live through it. He swore that he would never go to prison again. And so he became a free robber."

"Oh, so that's how it was! Daniel," I asked again, "do you also know the under ox drover that Knapp attacked?"

The chief hand looked at me in utter surprise. His eyes were amused. "You could be the son of the mayor," he said. "You're a regular sly one. What thoughts you have!"

He stood up, but before leaving, he said, "Of course I know the under ox drover. His father has enough trouble with him. That time-waster is bone lazy. The only thing he works hard at is drinking and playing cards."

Frau Knapp's Tears

THE FOLKS AT THE MAYOR'S FARM not only woke
with the chickens, they went to bed with them. People who
don't have chickens don't understand why this is. But it's
very simple. Hens roost in the coop when it gets dark. And
what's right for chickens isn't so wrong for people, either.
For instance, how would I get up the stairs to my bed in total
darkness? There was only one lantern in the kitchen, and it
had to stay there in case someone had to go to the barn at
night because an animal was sick or giving birth. So I preferred to go to my room while there was still some light left.

That night I couldn't get to sleep. There was a spooky
unrest in the house. People came and went. Doors opened
and closed. Scraps of sentences, sometimes clear, sometimes
muffled, floated up to my bed. It was like the moment before
a storm when lightning flashes.

I heard Uncle talking, but it was his mayor's voice. He was

speaking officialese. Normal people don't talk that way, they just write documents that way.

The schoolmaster had the most to say.

I opened the door to my room so I could listen to some of it.

The minister spoke and then some of the village councilors. What was so important that it had to be discussed at night? I strained to hear.

Fuenfkorn was sent away.

"Bring me Knapp's wife. Quickly!" I heard the mayor say, and then came the world-famous *"Exakt!"* of the police constable.

I became alert. So it had to do with the Knapps.

The schoolmaster was talking loud enough so that I could understand. "This is sure to help, Herr Mayor!" he exclaimed. "We'll give him an ultimatum—until tomorrow night—and if Knapp doesn't give himself up, his children will be taken away from him. It's our duty as Christians to take charge of the children of the robber family and see that they are brought up respectably."

Aha! So the schoolmaster had concocted a plan. This was what he had thought was so important before that he had to have a private meeting with the mayor during supper. Dreadful things were happening tonight.

Then the minister said, "The children always go to church, and they are not at all bad. But if it must be, then let it be, in God's name!"

Frau Knapp was brought in. Fuenfkorn said, "Order executed! *Exakt!*"

Apparently they all went into the kitchen or into the office.

I heard only murmuring and buzzing, punctuated by the energetic voice of the mayor.

Then I heard a woman weeping and wailing. It had to be Frau Knapp. Suddenly she shrieked. Had she been abandoned by God and all good spirits and lost her reason?

"Criminals! Miserable criminals!" she cried. Half the village must have heard her, and I was shaken by the inhuman voice. "Curses be on you, you damned child robbers!"

Tumult. First the office door opened and closed loudly, then the kitchen door opened and closed. My uncle—no, the *mayor*—cried sharp and loud, "In the name of the king!"

What was he doing in the name of the king? Soon I knew. The front door opened and closed. A woman was shrieking and crying in the yard. Frau Knapp. The jail door clanged shut and was locked. And because she continued to wail and bellow in there, the heavy shutters over the windows were closed and fastened with a heavy bar.

I couldn't get to sleep for a long time. The goosefeathers lay doubly heavy on me. I was worried about Christian. What would happen to him and to his family?

The church tower clock struck three. Frau Knapp was still shrieking. Then I fell into a foggy hole. Of course the only dreams I had were bad ones. The mayor, the minister, and schoolmaster grabbed a howling woman and several children by the hair and dragged them through the village.

Euenfkorn's Duty

BY EARLY MORNING, the whole village knew the story. Knapp's wife was having her children taken away from her.

Frederika was very upset. "Of course I'm almost positive that the mayor will make everything right," she said at breakfast. "But," she added, "I could weep if I thought of the Knapp children as my own." She wiped her eyes, reached for my head, took it between her pot-lid hands, and pressed it to her.

"Boy," she said very tenderly, "be glad that you have a rich uncle." Then she added softly, "And me!"

A person really had to like Frederika. I was about to tell her so.

"Why?" asked Daniel. "Why are they doing this? The Knapp children are neat, always clean. They don't do anything to anybody. They go to school, and to church on Sundays. Why don't they leave them with their mother?"

The mayor said nothing.

I didn't like Uncle that morning, and so I didn't look at him at all. I hoped he noticed!

Beadle and Police Constable Fuenfkorn came into the kitchen. He barely saluted. "Mayor!" he said. "I'm off, then. It must be done. The ultimatum for Knapp is pointless now. Therefore I'll be taking the children to their new lodgings this morning." At the door he turned once again. "Allow me to respectfully point out that I am only carrying out an order." Then he exited like an ordinary man and not like the respectable personage of the police constable.

The mayor called him back. "When you have carried out your duty, come back here at once and report!"

The constable didn't say *moo* and he didn't say *baa* and not even once did he say *"Exakt!"* That had to mean something. He didn't even say "Yessir!" which was his second most important word. In the mayor's house everyone could see that the beadle and police constable was in a very bad way.

Christian was not in school. I didn't see the girl with the braid down to her behind either. I hoped she wasn't sick.

I couldn't stop thinking about Christian all morning. This would be a hard time for him. To whom would the village bigwigs sell him off?

They were already sitting down to dinner at the mayor's house when I got home from school. They had waited to eat until I came. Certainly Frederika was responsible for that. She liked me a lot. I liked her too. When the right time comes, I thought, I really must tell her so.

Police Constable Fuenfkorn was also sitting there, and

Christian. I was delighted. No, I wasn't allowed to sit next to him.

"You will sit by me, and Knapp will sit down with the farmhands!" Uncle decreed.

Carefully I stole a glance at Christian. He looked very sad. That was no surprise. Just then, Frederika put a piece of meat on his plate. She was nice to him, and that was reassuring.

After the meal Frederika got a jug of cider out of the cellar. She offered it to Fuenfkorn.

"Well, Fuenfkorn, let's hear your report!" the mayor commanded. To me and the servants he said, "You can stay here. You can hear this; it's not an official secret!"

Fuenfkorn poured down a stomachful of cider and then began to talk.

"Mayor!" he began, "I don't ever want to do anything like that again. It could ruin my whole religion. The eyes of the children follow me, and they will haunt me for who knows how long. . . . So, I went very early to house number nine, where all the Knapp children were lodged alone. Their mother is in jail, of course."

Fuenfkorn took three swigs of cider.

"Everyone knows that little house, but you only discover how small it really is when you're inside it for the first time. It's only one room and a kitchen. All four children sleep in one bed. The big ones at the bottom, the two little ones at the top. Where does Frau Knapp sleep when she's home? All five must be in the one bed, because there isn't a second one. There isn't any room for one.

"I thought the kids would blubber the place down when I opened the door. But they didn't! They only stared at me, and there was a heap of fear in their big eyes. They didn't cry one little bit. Probably Schoolmaster Altmayer was right when he said poor children can't cry."

The beadle and police constable wiped the sweat off his face, gulped down a large quantity of cider, and continued talking.

"I was going to take Wilhelmine first. The little mite couldn't even walk properly and I had to carry her. I hope she stays dry, I thought. It was lucky the kid was only going four doors down to the parish officer.

" 'Come!' I said, not very loud. I didn't want to scare anyone. It was dead still in the room, and not one of the children moved. 'Come, Wilhelmine! You have to go!' I couldn't think of anything better to say. 'What must be, must be!' I said. It made me feel awful. I had such a bad conscience that it hurt my stomach. I made it snappy, picked up Wilhelmine, and hurried out onto the street.

"There was no crying, no screaming. Wilhelmine lay there quietly in my arms, and the other three stayed just as quiet. They were all standing behind me, and as I turned around, I again saw their huge, anxious eyes. I began to walk and to sweat, and the three Knapp children followed me."

Beadle and Police Constable Fuenfkorn swallowed a few times, then continued his report.

"We stopped in front of the house of the parish officer. With one hand I held the child, with the other I knocked on the front door. The wife of the parish officer came out. She was annoyed and fussed about my bad manners. Without a word I thrust little Wilhelmine into her arms. Then I crossed the street and went into the Crown."

Fuenfkorn interrupted his report. Something was stuck in his throat. He washed it down with cider, then continued.

"As you know, Mayor, I almost never drink on duty. But this morning I needed something. No human being could get through this otherwise. So, I went into the Crown. 'David,' I gasped to the barkeeper, 'quick, give me a pear brandy.'

"Next I collected eight-year-old Gottfried. The Knapp children were back in the house again. Without another word I took the boy by the hand and, without looking around, I went through the upper village, past the store, to the Goetzenbronn, over the wet meadows, and up the hill to Morbach. The two Knapp children were panting along behind me. I never turned around, so as not to have to meet their eyes.

"The old weaver shuffled out after I pounded and called. 'Weberbauer and his wife aren't home,' he grumbled, 'and they won't be back anytime soon.' He didn't know anything about a boy, he mumbled, and what would he want with a boy. He hadn't asked for one, and so he wouldn't take one. 'To the devil with him!' he yelled. So I took Gottfried by the arm again, and we hurried back to the village. The two Knapp children were still right behind me."

Constable Fuenfkorn stopped. The sweat was simply pouring off his bald head and down his face. He wiped it away with his sleeve. Didn't he have a handkerchief? Per-

haps it was so dirty it couldn't be used anymore. He continued his report.

"I rested in the Poorhouse for a bit because the walking and hurrying had used up a lot of wind. 'Now it's your
turn,' I said to eleven-year-old Karolyn. 'You're going to rich
Farmer Gayer over toward Schoenbronn,' I said. 'You'll
have it good there!' But I was looking at a crack in the floor-
board as I talked so I wouldn't have to look at the girl,
because I myself didn't believe what I was saying.

"I hurried to Schoenbronn along the church path in the
lake meadow. I never got there so quickly before. The two
other Knapp children were behind us. I've rarely perspired
so much. Nevertheless I was cold to my very bones. . . .
Gayer saw us coming. He watched us from a distance. When
we arrived he practically snatched the girl out of my hands
and he said that Karolyn had to go right into the kitchen to
start cleaning and cooking.

"I started back immediately. I don't like Gayer, can't stand
him at all, and if I stayed only a second too long, I would
have probably knocked him to the ground. Which, as a
police constable, I'm not allowed to do. So there was nothing
to do but get out of there. The two Knapp children were
behind me. I just kept hearing them panting and gasping,
because I didn't trust myself to turn around. I refused to look
into their eyes!"

The police constable poured more cider down his throat,
and he didn't stop until his stomach was full up to the rim.
How much cider would fit into this man? He wiped his
mouth and continued.

"Back to Morbach again. With eight-year-old Gottfried. Again the long walk to Goetzenbronnen and up the steep meadow slope. I was almost done in. Young Christian was always behind me. This time Weberbauer and his old lady were home. They're very decent, and they immediately gave Gottfried something to eat and drink and gave me two pear brandies."

Thus ended Constable Fuenfkorn's report, as there was no cider left in the jug. He stood up and saluted to anyone and no one.

"Now that I've delivered Christian Knapp here, I have carried out the order. I also respectfully report that I, Fuenf-korn, want to have nothing to do with this. Nothing, nothing at all. I have only carried out an order."

It was still as a mouse in the mayor's kitchen.

I didn't dare breathe.

Outside the birds were twittering all around, and the bull in the stall was rattling the chain that ended at his nose. The early summer sun beamed in through the window, shining so nicely and amiably that it would seem all the world must be rejoicing. But no one in the mayor's house was rejoicing. How could you?

Frederika sniffled, Daniel was openly shaking his head, and the others around the table were staring off into space, stunned.

Uncle's Word Is Law

IT HAD SNOWED once again during the night. The wet, soft snow lay heavy on the meadows, flowers, bushes, and trees, pressing the tender spring flowers to the ground. I hoped they would survive.

The road was nothing but slush. The cold, ice-watery mush leaked into the holes in shoe soles and through the eyes for shoelaces. Feet got soaking wet and cold.

The schoolhouse smelled musty, of damp clothes and unwashed children. Of course the stove wasn't lit, and so the bad air hung in the room for the entire morning. But with time, noses get used to any stench. Eighty boys and girls sneezed into damp, dirty handkerchiefs.

The girl with the braid was back again. She coughed constantly and terribly.

During recess I tried to get near her. Recess was just

pushing and shoving. In this awful weather no one went down to the street. We all stayed in the classroom.

Then I managed it. I was standing directly behind the girl. The beautiful, long braid was close enough to grab. I intended only to touch it a bit by accident. Nothing else. I got very hot, and my heart did a somersault. The girl coughed.

Suddenly Christian Knapp shoved in between us. What did he want just at that moment? It was no accident. I looked at the intruder angrily. What did he care if I got too close to the girl?

He looked me in the face, and the girl also turned around to me. Six eyes stared at each other. Then I saw it. The face of the girl was the face of Christian, and the other way around.

Oh, so that was it! I was really a giant ox not to have noticed it immediately. That's why the girl was always crying when the schoolmaster picked on Christian.

To make matters worse, Christian asked me very angrily, "What do you want with my sister Karolyn? Keep your hands off her! Or you'll have to deal with me!"

"I don't want anything at all!" I said and pushed back to my place. The name suited her, and really I was overjoyed that she was Christian's sister and that he watched over her so carefully. Then something else struck me: This Karolyn was the Knapp girl that the constable had taken to the disagreeable Gayer in Schoenbronn. Oh dear! That wasn't good at all.

Christian remained in the mayor's house. The church convention had decided it. They said the mayor was the only one in the village who could deal with this rebellious fellow. The schoolmaster had prophesied that within two weeks Christian Knapp would be eating out of the mayor's hand. Was he right?

Frederika had tried once more at the midday meal. She had placed Christian's spoon beside mine and remarked, a little fearfully, "The boys belong together."

Uncle's eyes were hard and unrelenting. "I don't wish it, and therefore, once and for all, that's the end of it!"

I already knew that once Uncle said, "That's the end of it," it was decreed until Judgment Day.

It was like church around the dinner table. Only somewhat quieter. Except for the usual smacking and slurping and clattering of spoons, there weren't any unnecessary sounds.

Maid Frederika grew red in the face, and then she couldn't contain herself. "A funeral is more cheerful than this!" she said with a reproachful look around the table at her dinner companions. Then, as if frightened by her own courage, she added apologetically, "I only just thought!"

Then it was quiet at the table again. Old Daniel cast an almost friendly look toward Christian now and then, but it was also full of concern. Uncle acted as if Christian weren't even there. His face was as stern and unreadable as always.

Christian just sat there, not looking left, not looking right, not looking straight ahead. He sat there as if he and his present surroundings did not exist. Perhaps he was somewhere else entirely, or nowhere.

God often has some very complicated ideas, and for many

a man He ordains a difficult and weary detour to heaven. Christian certainly belonged to those with the greatest detour. Someday he was going to get a really good place up there because he was so badly knocked around on earth. That surely had to be so. Because otherwise it would not only be hellishly unfair on earth but also in heaven.

Life in the mayor's house had become very stressful since the robber's son Christian had arrived. I'd been living under the same roof with him since yesterday, and that really ought to have been very nice. We liked each other. Uncle could have had another bed put in my garret, and if necessary there was even enough room in my bed. But I wasn't even allowed to talk with Christian. Uncle had forbidden it. So I had to treat him like a godless heathen or a plowhorse. A heathen isn't a human being as long as he isn't converted, and you only say *gee* and *haw* to a plowhorse.

That evening I was alone in the kitchen with Frederika. She had told Uncle that she needed me urgently. But I thought she'd noticed my swirling thoughts and wanted to talk with me about them. I got four armloads of wood out of the shed and two buckets of water from the well and emptied the ash box out over the dung heap. Afterwards I had to scrub off the black on the potato pot with sand. Frederika never had any time for anything else than her work. She slaved and provided and was busy the entire day. She only interrupted her work for eating and sleeping and another small matter. Nevertheless, she now sat down across from me.

"Boniface," she said. "I see it in you. You have a few troubling thoughts locked up in your head. Let them out!"

I did like Frederika. She always knew what I was thinking and what was bothering me.

"Frederika," I asked, "what's going to happen with Christian?"

"Boy, if I only knew!"

"Frederika, how should I act with Christian? He hasn't done me any harm, and I even like him. How can I treat him like a dog! No, even worse! I could at least pet a dog, but I'm not even allowed to look at Christian."

Frederika thought for a long time, and three thick furrows formed in her brow. Then she opened her mouth so wide that her back teeth showed. It was her soundless laugh. I was already familiar with that!

"Tough, very tough!" she said slyly. "Of course your uncle's word is law. You absolutely must obey him. Obviously. And without talking back! But . . ." Frederika hesitated for a long moment. Then, with an apologetic glance at the kitchen ceiling, she whispered the words of rescue: "What did your uncle say? Didn't he say he didn't want to see you with Christian Knapp anymore? Very well, Boniface. He said *see*. Then you must be very careful that he doesn't see you. Your uncle has only two eyes, and they can't be everywhere."

Naturally I didn't understand Frederika right away. It took me a while, because I'm not particularly clever. But at last I got the idea.

I liked Frederika. How smart she was. I wanted to give

her a big kiss on the cheek, but I didn't dare. She was blush-
ing a little now, as if she read my thoughts.

After three days Frau Knapp was free again. She ran up to
Morbach three times a day, and just as often to Schoenbronn,
because she absolutely had to see her children. In between
she loitered in front of the mayor's house and the house of
the parish officer.

When would she go crazy? Perhaps she already had.

A Black Cat

THE JAIL WAS OCCUPIED AGAIN.

"Who's the pretty young woman in there now?" I asked Frederika.

"Dear God," she said. "That's another poor, unfortunate mite—Ulrike, the daughter of Alwine Fratz. She's in there because of fornication, and it's her third time already."

"What's 'because of fornication'?"

"Well, that's not something to be explained so easily or quickly."

Frederika hesitated, frowned, and then said to me, "You're big enough now to be able to understand it. So pay attention! Ulrike is going to have a baby. You can tell that from her big belly. But a woman is only allowed to have a baby when she's married. And because Ulrike Fratz isn't, she must have engaged in fornication. Babies don't come all by themselves. The father of the child is Day Laborer Klein's son. This is the third child she's had by him. Fratz and Klein, they've known each other since they were children, and they like each other. And they would gladly marry, but they aren't allowed to, because they can't get permission. The mayor won't allow it. Their livelihood isn't secure, they say."

"What's a livelihood?" I asked.

"Livelihood? Oh, well, it's just that. So that a future married couple doesn't become a burden on the parish, they have to be able to show they have some property. A farm, for example, with so many cows, or a smithy, or some other trade. Or two hundred gulden. A day laborer's son naturally doesn't have a farm and usually isn't able to learn a trade, because that also costs a lot of money. He also won't inherit anything, for his father doesn't have anything of his own to leave him. And two hundred gulden? That is a terrific lot of money. Where would he get that kind of money?"

"His savings," I said thoughtfully.

"Oh, boy! By the time a young fellow who works as a day laborer or a maid could save two hundred gulden, they would be old and gray, and then they would still be a hundred short."

Frederika stopped for a long time. Then she sighed. "Yes, that's how it is for poor people. Because they're poor, they aren't allowed to marry, and so the children come into the world out of wedlock. But children out of wedlock have been created through fornication, and for that reason the poor mother must go to jail."

"Why the mother? Why don't they lock up the father?"

"Ah, boy. The girl's always the one who's indecent. She's the one who has the child."

"But that's horribly unfair."

"How true it is! But what's fair in our world?"

"Frederika, tell me, why is my uncle so against the poor people that he won't let them marry?"

"Your uncle can't do anything about it. This is the law of the entire kingdom."

I was a little relieved to hear that my uncle was not entirely to blame.

"People shouldn't have to be poor at all!" I said to Frederika.

"Yes, that would be best."

I left Frederika and got a beautiful red apple out of the storeroom in the cellar and laid it on the sill of the jail window.

By now I had been living in Graab for thirty-seven days.

My uncle and the minister had decided that I should be friends with Albert. Naturally any friend was all right with me, especially if he was the minister's son. But twelve-year-old Albert was as silly as a seven-year-old, and he only behaved well when any other people were watching him. The rest of the time he talked about people behind their backs and he farted and he did everything that his father condemned in his sermons. I didn't want to have anything to do with him. I wouldn't like him even if they beat me. Why didn't Uncle let me be friends with Christian?

Today was Easter Saturday, the great washday. It wasn't clothes that were washed but people. First the men, then the women.

A nice lineup: Uncle, the chief farmhand, the young hand, Christian, and me, then Frederika, the older under maid, and finally the young under maid. Normally I would have come right after my uncle because I belonged to family. But Frederika wanted it otherwise. I came just before her because she wanted to scrub me thoroughly.

First a huge quantity of wood was carried into the laundry kitchen, and water, lots of water. Enormous quantities of water had to be carried in. All the buckets were in use. The big kettle had to be kept steaming. When the water was hot, it was poured into the washtub, and the person sat or lay down in it. Each person had about an hour. That was enough time for even the most resistant dirt to soften. More than a pound of soap was used up on such a wash day, so I suppose it was economical for baths not to be taken very often.

No one else was allowed to go into the laundry kitchen when someone was bathing, because the person in the tub was completely naked. Everyone was afraid of nakedness. Why, I didn't know. Frederika said people were just embarrassed.

I took my bath just before the noonday meal. Frederika scrubbed me thoroughly, and afterwards I still didn't know what the embarrassment was all about. I was given a fresh shirt and clean trousers. Everyone from the mayor's house smelled of soap the whole day. Even the chief hand, Daniel, had a completely strange scent.

On Easter Sunday the Devil himself came to the village.

On such a great feast day the sermon took its time. It was about the resurrection of creation. I didn't quite know what the minister meant, but I didn't need to follow every detail. After all, the minister wasn't preaching for me alone; surely there were some in the church who understood what he was saying.

The door was wide open because of the beautiful Easter Sunday sun and the twittering of the birds and the fresh air. The air was urgently required. Otherwise, more people than just Johann Georg Schaefer and Gottlob Kienle would fall asleep, and that wouldn't be good for the sermon, because most of them snored.

Suddenly the Devil stood there at the open door. He looked like a black cat. The minister saw him first because he was the only one who could see the door. When he stopped short in the middle of a sentence with shock and gazed at the door, speechless, I and the rest of the congregation turned to see what was there.

A cat was standing at the center of the doorway. But what a cat! Who had ever seen such a coal-black cat? There were plenty of cats in Graab: one-colored, two-colored, three-colored, tiger-striped, black-spotted, gray, and all white. But nobody had ever seen a black cat.

Had the minister not just mentioned the name Satan? There he was now! As if summoned! The cat-devil howled into the startled silence. It didn't meow like a normal cat but more like a bewitched child or a three-week-old piglet whose snout has just been trampled by the mother sow.

Police Constable Fuenfkorn restored order. He strode fearlessly, like Saint George the Dragon Slayer, up to the cat-devil and banished it from the church.

But that was only the beginning.

On Easter Monday it hailed. The flowers couldn't tolerate something like that at this point. Someone or other had seen the black cat just before it started. Like wildfire the news spread through the village. The cat-devil had brought the hail. On the same day, Leonhard Krafft's little Eugenie came down with quinsy and someone or other had seen the child petting the black cat just before that.

The boys and young men armed themselves with sticks and large stones and went on a cat hunt.

Of course Uncle was angry. This was silly nonsense; a cat was no devil. I was of the same opinion as Uncle, which was quite rare. Naturally the poor animal had nothing to do with Beelzebub. But it *was* funny that such a black animal had just casually appeared in the village like that and nobody knew where it came from. And the howling was also quite strange. A normal cat rarely howls so heartbreakingly.

The young fellows searched the entire village for the cat-devil. They intended to destroy the Satan, and they would have done so had the black cat not vanished from the earth.

Devil's Ditch

EASTER MONDAY was an important school day. It took place in the church, and the entire village was there. The minister talked, then the mayor, and finally the schoolmaster. I didn't need to pay attention to anything, because none of it was worth it.

At first the lower class showed what they had learned. The little boys and girls were terribly excited, and they often got mixed up. Then we, the upper class, recited in front of the entire congregation in beautiful order, and it went like clockwork. A few weak heads were skipped over entirely, but hardly anyone noticed.

The schoolmaster read out the report cards, and the fathers and mothers were either proud, or they slid down in the pews as far as they could so that no one would see them.

The children of the schoolmaster were graded *good*, in all categories, as were the minister's three children and I. That was as it should be, and there was no better grade than *good*. The two boys of Village Councilor Bay weren't as clever as we. They received only four *good*s, a *fairly good*, and a *diligent*. Day laborers' children were *average* or *not remarkable*, and the robber's son, Christian Knapp, was *very bad*. It was certainly a piece of luck that his father wasn't sitting in the pew. Only Frau Knapp was there to feel ashamed of her dumb, lazy, and recalcitrant son.

On the way home I happened to overhear Farmer Leonhard Deininger say to his wife that it couldn't go on that way with their children's grades. It was just too shameful. Their neighbors' two boys always got at least two *good*s, and they only had four more cows in their barn than the Deiningers. And the neighbor was only a village councilor. "Wife," he said, "we must change that! The fields belonging to Carl Friedrich Klenk's widow have just been put up for sale. I'll buy them, and then I can keep at least four more cows in the barn. Then there'll be the devil to pay if after that Konrad and Adam don't get *good*s also."

If you considered it from all sides, being an orphan boy, I hadn't fared at all badly. I was lucky that my uncle was mayor of Graab. There was no difficulty with the grades. I could hardly picture my uncle, the mayor, sliding down in the first pew because he was ashamed in front of the whole parish.

Easter Monday was not only a school day, but also the last shoe day. From that day forward all the children went barefoot. I ended up every evening with my feet in the cold pump trough because Frederika wouldn't let me go to bed with cow dung between my toes. The schoolmaster could easily search for dirty feet now, but, strangely enough, he didn't do it.

The days after Easter were nicely mixed: a little rain, abundant sun, mild nights. Accordingly, the greenery shot out of the ground. In the meadows there appeared thousands and thousands of dandelions. They colored everything egg-yolk yellow.

A few days later I learned something else: Christian Knapp sneaked out of the house at night. When he was done with his work, he always went to pee at the dung heap, and then suddenly he was gone. Usually it was already dusk or completely dark when he stole away. Probably no one had noticed yet. The young farmhand, in whose room Christian slept, naturally had no idea, for he was seldom home at night. He said that he met with the village lads. But Daniel knew better, from a reliable source. He said the young hand was cuddling with a certain young village beauty.

What was keeping Christian out so late?

Today, after supper, I stayed in the kitchen with Frederika, so I was the first to notice when Knapp left the house. The mayor had gone back into his office with a gigantic frown over his eyes. Frederika also wasn't particularly talkative. Instead of talking to me she grumbled to herself. Why? Nobody knew exactly. Maybe she didn't know herself. She was always finding reasons to gripe. It could be because of some unkind village gossip, or because of last Sunday's sermon. Or a story out of the *Little Garden of Eden* or the *Soul's Apothecary*. Frederika kept these two pious little books in her trunk. She had probably read the stories in them hundreds of times, and now and again she would discover a new thought there. She said that a person must read something now and again or he would stay dumb and even lose the little bit he knew from his school days. Sometimes Frederika grumbled about Napoleon. He was to blame for her grandfather's death when he was a mere twenty-six years old. He had drowned in the icy waters of Beresina in November of 1812 during the retreat from Russia.

Aha! Now someone was stealing down the stairs. No matter how carefully you stepped, those wooden stairs creaked. Certainly it was Christian! Who else?

I wished Frederika good night and hurried out. Yes, indeed, it was Christian. He relieved himself at the dung heap. Then he looked around. He didn't see me, because I was standing in the dark doorway. He went out of the yard, walked to the lake meadow, and on to the edge of the forest. What was he going to do at the edge of the forest at nightfall?

There was no proper path through there. The forest began with the three big oaks, and right next to them, between the trees, lay the notorious Devil's Ditch. Nobody went there after the sun went down. People told the creepiest, scariest stories about the ditch. What was said to have happened in the ditch was simply beyond belief: Red, green, and white lights flitted across it; shrill screams, sorrowful howling, and pain-filled groaning broke the silence of the night; strange forms that couldn't be identified as man or beast hovered over it; people who had been murdered or had died of fear whined there for their release. So it was said in the village. Everyone had once seen or heard this, that, or the other thing, and finally no one knew anymore what he'd seen for himself and what he only knew from hearsay.

For instance, there was the story of old Gottlieb Albert Drei. It didn't even come directly from him because he'd already been dead for years. I heard it from Frederika, who hadn't heard it from Drei either but from someone who'd heard it from yet another person. The story changed a little each time, because Frederika always remembered it slightly differently. But what difference does that make?

Gottlieb Albert Drei used to be a regular at the Stag. He would always go there when he had a few kreuzer in his pocket. One evening, after four beers, and because it was midnight, the Stag's barkeeper had thrown him out. Now something strange happened, and Drei ought to have been suspicious. But that's the way it is when a person has a beer fog in his head—he could no longer use his brain, small as it was. A strange hiker was standing in front of the Stag. You might wonder about a hiker at that hour! Exactly at midnight. The stranger said to Drei, "Come with me. I'll make you rich!" And because Drei, in his foggy state, couldn't tell the difference anymore between a hiker and the Devil, he went with him. This man, who was no man, led Drei out of the village, straight to the edge of the field, and to the big, thick oak by Devil's Ditch. At exactly the spot where the ruins of a tower are today, he stopped and scratched his foot against the ground so that the sparks flew. Drei was terribly frightened. He saw without any doubt that the strange hiker had a billy goat's hoof instead of a human foot. After the shower of sparks and the stink of sulfur had vanished into the forest, Drei caught sight of a chest filled with glowing gold pieces on the bottom of Devil's Ditch. The hiker—no, for now even Drei knew that before him stood Beelzebub in person—said in a spiteful voice, "Take the gold, it belongs to you!" Drei, who had never seen a gold piece in his entire life, was blinded. He reached into the chest and played with all that gold. "You must only sign this contract with me, then all the gold belongs to you!" said the Prince of Darkness coaxingly. And because Drei had led a bitterly poor life all his days, he wanted to have it easier during his last years. He took the contract. But first he questioned the Devil. "What's it say?" asked Drei. "What's in it? I can't read."

"Not much," said the Devil. "Only the one thing: gold for your soul!"

"Oh, woe!" whispered Drei. But then he considered the things he could buy with all that gold: the entire village of Graab or the Limpurger Castle in Gaildorf; all he could eat and drink at the Stag every day; anything his heart desired. Even the rich farmers would take off their hats to him because he would be even richer than they were. What was there to consider for very long? Drei said, "Yes, I'll do it!" All on account of a chest filled with gold. The Devil grabbed a coal-black crow that was flying past, pulled a feather out of it, stuck one of Drei's fingers with it until it bled, dipped the feather in it, and pressed it into Gottlieb Albert Drei's hand. Drei took the contract and the crow's feather and signed the deal. But since Drei had never learned to read, he was, of course, also unable to write. He couldn't even put together the four letters of his name. So he just made his usual three crosses on the paper. Then! . . . A crash like a lightning bolt, a stench like a fart, and the illusion vanished entirely. They say that the Devil can tolerate everything, but not three crosses. So Drei was lucky once more, and, as you see, sometimes it can even be a good thing if a person can't write his name. The next morning Drei was safe and sound, though he was lying under the oak with a thundering headache. He couldn't explain how he got there. Yet he could never get the adventure with the Devil out of his head, either. He dug one hole after the other in Devil's Ditch but found nothing. Frederika knew from a reliable source that later Drei had even learned, with much difficulty, to write his name. In case the Devil ever passed by there again. But the Devil very wisely decided not to. Meanwhile, Drei died. Frederika had known him. He was a poor swine all his life, she said. Like her grandfather, he'd been dragged to Moscow with Napoleon. He was the only Graab man to make it back. He didn't say much about Russia, but once, when he was especially drunk, he let it out: There'd been such terrible hunger on the retreat that they ate comrades who had frozen to death.

"The story of Gottlieb Albert Drei and the Devil is a good example of why you must always be on your guard!" said Frederika.

Who would want to be carried off to hell some night by some clever trick of the cloven-hoofed one, with no return, forever and ever? It was best to avoid all the places where the

Devil loitered. Or only go there in the daytime when the Devil was bothering people on the other side of the earth, where it was midnight.

What was Christian Knapp doing in such a haunted place?

It wasn't really proper night yet; it was only just getting dark. In short bursts I sneaked after the shadow. He mustn't catch sight of me, and I mustn't lose him. The edge of the forest swallowed him. Was he waiting there, or had he gone farther in among the trees?

Now I was at a disadvantage. He could see me, but I couldn't see him. Therefore I made an arc around the oaks and Devil's Ditch and slipped into the forest beside it. There I waited and listened. Slowly, the last daylight faded.

Today I was going to find out the secret of Christian Knapp!

Carefully I tiptoed to Devil's Ditch, step by step. Naturally I was afraid. Not so much of the Devil, for he certainly had more important things to do than to lie in wait for me—and who knew if he really existed anyway? My father was of the opinion that the Devil was the wickedness in the world and not a childish masquerader, as he was often depicted in church.

Wasn't Christian afraid? If he wasn't, I wasn't.

Two birds squawked excitedly. Was it just two half-grown thrushes arguing, or was a sentinel warning the rest of the forest of intruders?

Then, where the embankment must be, I heard a man's low voice. I started. Was there such a thing as a Devil's Ditch spirit? And then a stone fell from my heart. Christian called softly, "Here I am, by the big oak!" But immediately anxiety petrified me again. The man was certainly Robber Knapp, Christian's father. So he met with him every evening! I was also a little disappointed. This secret wasn't particularly mysterious. I ought to have figured it out sooner.

It would be best to get back! Before the robber caught me or Christian recognized me. All at once I had a very bad conscience. How could I be so mistrustful and curious about a friend? At the edge of the forest I went quietly from tree to tree.

A man with a large hat emerged from the embankment of Devil's Ditch. Of course! That was Robber Knapp. He was described that way by everyone, and that was the way I had seen him in my dream. He went a few paces into the meadow. Christian leapt out of the forest. "Father!" he said joyfully. And Knapp took him and tossed him up a good way into the air. How strong the man was! He caught him skillfully again, and now something quite incredible happened. Christian remained hanging on the neck of the robber, and in the half dark the two of them looked as if they were one.

They were standing a few paces in front of me in the meadow.

Stars began appearing. More and more of them. The dew trickled over my bare feet. It was pleasantly cold between my toes and around my ankles. Then a fierce pain stabbed my left foot like a stinging nettle. Some passing forest ant must have felt itself threatened and pinched me on the leg. I had to scratch.

Just don't also have to cough now! And as I thought that, my throat was already tickling. Drat! A cough arises when your throat is dry or an imaginary gnat is stuck in your gullet. So I collected my spit and let it slowly run down my throat. It helped, but only for a short time. So I repeated the procedure several times and the dry cough tickle was dampened for a while. Then there was no moisture left in my head. I pressed my throat. In vain. I had to cough. I barked into the night several times. Then everything happened very fast. Before I could hide, the robber had grabbed me, and Christian was standing right next to him.

"It's only a little fellow!" said Knapp, and he appeared relieved.

"That's Boniface Schroll," said Christian.

"Hey, are you Schroll? I already know you. Well, but today you look entirely different. Where's your hair? I took you for a girl when I found you whimpering in the forest."

"What are you doing at Devil's Ditch so late?" Christian asked me.

I thought it would be terribly wrong if I tried to lie my way out. Therefore I told it the way it was: "I sneaked after you, because I was curious about what you were doing in this dangerous corner of the forest at this hour. If I'd known that you were meeting your father . . ."

"It doesn't matter!"

I was ashamed, and I pulled myself together and ran straight back to the mayor's house.

I lay sleepless for a long time under my goosefeathers. Now I knew for sure who was responsible for my not freezing to death that night in the forest. Knapp was the man who had found me and carried me to Graab. And this man was supposed to be a wicked robber? I stopped believing it at that moment. I hadn't even thanked him, I reproached myself. I was a miserable piece of humanity; I didn't even have the minimum of manners.

It must be nice to be thrown up in the air by your father and be caught in his arms again!

Before I fell asleep I prayed to God to protect Knapp and Christian and to declare their opponents His enemies. Especially Schoolmaster Altmayer—God should treat him badly. But He should spare my uncle a little. I wasn't praying to the regular God but to my own who resides even farther up. We know each other better.

Haying Time

IN THE COUNTRY, school vacations are entirely different. They aren't arranged for the children or for the teachers or for anything else having to do with school. They're strictly for the benefit of the farmers, because at certain times in the year farmers need their children in the meadows and fields. Therefore, there's a week's vacation for the haying, two weeks for the grain harvest, and three weeks for the fall activities.

The haying was due to begin in the next few days. There were two things that were important: the grass and the weather. The grass had grown to be knee-high. It smelled strong and spicy and was full of juice. It wouldn't get any better. So now only the weather had to cooperate. Often the hay will rot because instead of the sun drying it, there's a lot of rain, Daniel said.

Therefore it's important to have someone who can correctly predict what the weather will be and also tell you if it will hold for three days. For some years the people of Graab had relied on old Stiefelbauer from Trauzenbach. He was at least eighty-five years old and as toothless as a baby. But he could tell the weather.

Daniel knew him very well. He said that no man could truly know the weather in advance. That would be interfering in God's work. But old Stiefelbauer was something very close to a weather prophet.

Why could Stiefelbauer predict the weather?

Because he was ancient and had the experience of so many seasons. In addition, he was tormented by gout. Gout was very important in this. Normally it tore his limbs apart so badly that he often didn't know if he should stand, sit, lie, or do nothing at all. But at the present time, his gout was so well behaved that he almost forgot he had it. A better guarantee of good weather there couldn't be. For extra security, old Stiefelbauer also took a reading from his rooster. This rooster had three kinds of cries: the warning to the chickens when the goshawk was circling; a commanding fuss when he wanted to impress the hens; and, finally, his good-weather crow.

But not just anyone was able to hear his good-weather crow, explained Daniel. For that you needed special ears. And apparently old Stiefelbauer had them. It seems he also smelled the weather—which was even more peculiar, Daniel said, because old Stiefelbauer usually couldn't smell himself anymore. Anyway, when all the important signs for the hay harvest agreed, old Stiefelbauer sent his great-grandson to the mayor. And even though everyone knew what the messenger signified, the great-grandson would nevertheless be questioned. And he, with his chest puffed out with pride, would announce, "People, haying begins tomorrow!"

The next morning the schoolmaster banged his stick on his desk, signaling the beginning of the haying vacation. All 199 schoolchildren hurried to the fields surrounding the village of Graab and the outlying hamlets. There a hundred scythes had been cutting the dew-damp grass since early morning light. The big boys followed behind the mowers, raking the grass mounds apart so that the sun could reach as many blades as possible. The grass had to dry quickly and thoroughly. Now and then there would be a break. Some ate bread and bacon and pear cider, others just bread and water.

The church clock struck two o'clock, and everyone in the village and the surrounding area knew that it was one hour until noon. The women and girls returned home to cook. Meanwhile the sun sucked up moisture from the cut grass. It already smelled a little hayish.

Christian was with us in the meadow, too. He was assigned to Daniel, at the other end of the field. You could see that the work was easy for him, and to anyone who would listen Daniel mentioned that Christian was a diligent and useful lad.

That evening I was determined to get together with Christian. I had much to talk over with him. Something had occurred to me the night before, and things didn't fit together somehow. At the same time Knapp had found me in the forest, he had supposedly attacked the under ox drover in an entirely different place. That couldn't be. Either he was in one place or the other. I was going to tell Christian tonight. I was already looking forward to it.

Uncle insisted I work behind him all the time, in this way keeping me away from Christian. My uncle worked terribly fast, and after a short time I couldn't keep up with him anymore. My whole body hurt. Especially the palms of my hands. At first they were only hot, then a few blisters appeared. Soon they filled with water and burst. Apparently, no one else had this problem. I took out my handkerchief and wrapped it around one hand. That helped for a short time, but afterwards it was even worse. My hands were burning. It hurt the way it does when you accidentally brush your finger against the hot stove. I couldn't hold the rake any longer and laid it down in the grass.

If only Frederika were here! She would certainly help me. I looked at my hands. There was blood coming out of the blisters. Just don't cry, too!

Uncle looked back. "Where are you?" he called to me. Then he noticed my sore hands. He even looked at them for a brief moment. "You'll survive," he said, without sympathy. He gave me his handkerchief, then continued working.

I was so ashamed. Farmhands, day workers, the children of the day workers, and Christian noticed. Some laughed. The young farmhand said to the others, just loud enough for everyone to hear, "That city slicker isn't good for anything. He doesn't even earn the salt in his soup. But he eats like a stableboy. That he can do."

My uncle only glanced very quickly at the slanderer, who shut his mouth.

Why didn't I have hands like the others? Not even the smallest half-pint needed a handkerchief. And they worked the entire morning.

I wanted so much to be like Christian.

All the people around the young hand were giggling. I was sure they were laughing at me again.

Then, thank God, there was a distraction.

Beadle and Police Constable Fuenfkorn was hastening along the old Schoenbronn road. In one hand he carried his official cap, while with the other he kept wiping his sweaty, red face. Now he turned onto the path to the field. Yes, he was coming directly toward us. I knew that he didn't see particularly well—nothing up close and nothing in the distance. Therefore it took him a while before he could distinguish my uncle from the other people in the meadow. The beadle and police constable put on his uniform hat, assumed his official posture, and marched with official dignity up to the mayor. He clacked his shoes together and saluted.

"I beg to report, sir!"

"Report!"

"I beg to report, sir, that yesterday evening, at about dusk, Cattle Dealer Bofinger was walking from Laemmersbach to Altfuerstenhuette. *Exakt!*"

"Yes, and . . . ?"

"Bofinger met Herr Chief Forester Komerel in the middle of the forest, to the side of Oerlach, before the Roth runs across the Halle road. *Exakt!*"

"Yes, and what did Herr Chief Forester want?"

"He didn't want anything!"

"Yes, and so what is there to report?"

"*Exakt!* That comes next! As the cattle dealer was going on toward Altfuerstenhuette because of business he had there, he met someone else scarcely a hundred meters on."

"Yes, and whom did Bofinger meet there?"

"At first he didn't know either. *Exakt!* But when Bofinger saw that the other man was wearing a big black hat on his head and had a coal-black cloth over his face, he knew who the other man was."

"Yes, and who was it?"

"I beg to report, Mayor: Robber Knapp always has a black hat on his head. *Exakt!*"

"Yes, and did the robber do anything to Bofinger?"

"He didn't do anything to him. But he took from him exactly two hundred and ninety gulden."

"Yes, and did Bofinger just give him the money without a struggle?"

"He had to! Mayor, he had to! Because Robber Knapp held a pistol under his nose!"

"My God! That's going really too far!" My uncle was snorting with rage.

"Bofinger is waiting at your house to report the crime. And that's what I beg to report. *Exakt!*"

My uncle bore a great deal, and no one could read his thoughts in his face. But this report must have struck him deep in the heart. He stood there, supporting himself on his scythe, thinking. The sweat ran down his nose, onto the stubble on his upper lip, and from there onto his tongue. He probably didn't like the taste of the salty sweat. He tried to wipe it away with his sleeve. To do that, he took off his hat, because it was in the way. Now he could wipe his face unimpeded, but then the rays of the sun struck him right in the eyes. My uncle had a little trouble with his eyes. They couldn't tolerate bright light. Therefore Uncle turned so that his eyes were in the shade. But it looked as if he were turning just so that he could get Christian Knapp into his line of sight.

Christian Knapp noticed my uncle looking his way. He had certainly overheard Police Constable Fuenfkorn's loud report with his lynx ears. He, of course, knew that his father hadn't carried out a holdup yesterday. He was with him. Very quickly he looked over at me, as if to say "You know it too." But I felt as if I were nailed to boards, and so I said nothing.

Across the meadow Christian cried out, "Bofinger is lying! It wasn't my father!"

My uncle became upset. "Quiet, you miserable puppy!" he yelled angrily back across the meadow.

"Uncle," I said timidly, and I was going to say that I had seen Knapp yesterday at the big oak in Devil's Ditch at dusk and therefore he could not have been near Oerlach too.

"And you be quiet now!" my uncle snarled at me. I didn't dare say anything more.

Christian kept looking at me. I could have wept, for I was such a coward.

Then Christian Knapp threw down his rake in the field and fled into the forest.

The Storm

CHRISTIAN WAS GONE, and the beautiful weather went with him.

Someone said, "What times these are!" and another complained, "Stiefelbauer's weather is no good anymore either."

Old Daniel growled, "A person can't rely on anything or anybody these days. I guess old Stiefelbauer is just too old, or maybe the weather isn't playing by the old rules anymore. The world just isn't what it used to be."

In any case, big black clouds were now piling up in the east.

Whatever came from that direction was bad. There was no proper mountain in between. The storms would quickly reach Graab.

The farmers and hands and day workers and children—everyone, in fact, who had just been cutting hay—quickly shouldered their rakes and hurried home. A storm that approached from the Roth Valley was unpredictable. No one could tell ahead of time how long it would last and what harm it would do.

The grass was just starting to become hay. It was only half dry. Too bad! And it had all begun so well.

A few heavy drops fell, and the whole region turned a sulfurous yellow.

"Boniface! Run quickly!" Uncle called to me, and his voice contained a little concern. "Drop everything!"

I leaned the rake against an apple tree and ran with Uncle and the chief hand. Everyone was anxious and upset. The young hand and the day laborers' children were already back at the village. They could run faster.

The first lightning was already slamming down by Schoenbronn.

Uncle was groaning like Hexer, our parish bull. "The storm is catching up to us! Boy! Run as fast as you can!"

Was my uncle afraid for me?

I was wet down to my toenails when I reached the mayor's house. The air in my chest was all used up. Whole rivers were streaming off the roof.

Frederika was standing at the front door. "Get changed quickly! Otherwise you'll get the gout!" She made a cross in front of her face and breast every time the lightning flashed. Was she a Catholic? They did such things.

I leapt up the steps. Fast! Who could tell what the lightning had in mind? The mayor's house towered over the other houses in the district. Only the churchtower was higher. But it was far away.

I had to put on my Sunday trousers. The other pair was in the wash. It was pitch-dark in the garret. Except when the lightning flashed harsh and bright through the window. The roof panels rattled. The storm made them jump up and down, and sometimes the lightning showed through the cracks into the attic. It was leaking beside the bed.

Everyone was sitting together in the kitchen. Daniel was the last to come in. He wasn't so fast anymore. His old lungs gave him trouble. Whenever he had to strain especially hard, there was a rattle in his chest like a rusty chain and he gasped for air.

My uncle's face was serious. Such a severe thunderstorm was a bad thing, especially if it lingered up by the high field and didn't move on.

And if the lightning struck! Many a farmer has gone under from such a thing.

"Where can that poor Christian Knapp be?" Frederika said, uttering what I had been thinking the whole time. "He has nothing but his shirt and trousers."

"In this weather he'll catch his death!"

"Perhaps the lightning struck him!"

"Stop!" I cried. My throat was so full. There was nothing else for me to do, I had to cry.

"That's enough, now!" said my uncle angrily. "He has himself to blame! Why did he run off? No one did anything to him!"

Forcing it through the space between his last two bottom teeth, old Daniel said, "It's a crying shame what they're doing to the Knapps! Why are the children made to suffer?

And who knows whether it's true about Knapp?"

Daniel showed real anger in his face. He ground his stumps of teeth so that I was afraid they might break apart.

"A man should be certain of one thing before he comes into the world," he said. "Either he should slide out into this life well-to-do or he should stay where he is."

Frederika was nodding her head, as if to say that she thought exactly the same thing.

I wanted to make up for my cowardice, and so I placed myself in front of my uncle.

"Uncle!" I said.

I didn't get any further. A bolt of lightning struck very close by and a clap of thunder shook the house. Uncle leapt up. We looked out the window. The big pear tree beside the jail was shattered. The lightning bolt had split it into so many long splinters and crooked laths.

"That was close!" said Uncle.

"Oh-god-oh-god-oh-god!" wailed Frederika.

I pressed against Uncle. He was strong, he could protect me.

He looked at me and laid his hand on my shoulder, as if he wanted to hold me fast. But right away he took back his hand.

"What were you about to say?" he asked. "Yes, you, Boniface!" His voice was as unfeeling and hard as always. Then all my courage vanished, and I said to Uncle, "Oh, nothing! It wasn't important."

Again a lightning bolt struck close by, and again the chips flew.

"The old poplar at the weir!" cried the young hand.

"What a storm!" whimpered the under maid.

"Get away from the window!" called Frederika. "You shouldn't attract the lightning!"

I'd never experienced anything like it. There weren't storms like that in Cannstatt. My father once told me that a thunderstorm is nothing mysterious. It was only a few electrical sparks jumping back and forth. Well, those were quite some sparks!

Frederika saw how frightened I was. She took my head between her hands and stuck it under her apron.

Was I mistaken or did Uncle say, with quite some concern, "I hope nothing has happened to Christian Knapp"?

The Regiment

THERE WAS NO REAL HAPPINESS in the mayor's house.

Christian Knapp hadn't come back. Instead, a whole company of soldiers of the regiment of the Crown Prince at Ludwigsburg moved into the village. Without warning. My uncle was as cross as two sticks.

"This village has never seen so many strangers," said Frederika.

Maneuvers were going to be held in the local forest for an undetermined period.

"They're playing little soldier games!" said Daniel.

The school was requisitioned for military use. They needed it for the wounded, if there were any. Too bad it happened just now during the haying vacation. Next to the jail they set up a "goulash cannon"—a field kitchen. It smoked a lot and smelled good. Daniel knew about kitchens like that.

In a real war, he said, the horses that got shot were cooked into the goulash.

What excitement there was in the village. The young girls weren't allowed out of the house in the evenings anymore. Because the soldiers were said to be "ready to try anything."

Herr Captain was quartered with us. The young farmhand had to move into the barn. The mayor's office was now headquarters. The village was a war zone, the captain decreed, and this meant that the mayor was subject to his orders. This didn't please my uncle at all, and he spent all day looking in the royal laws and regulations for the place where it said that the mayor had to obey the military when maneuvers were taking place. Herr Captain was quite conceited and arrogant. He acted so secretive and chilly that my uncle said he felt as if he were not in his own house but deep in enemy territory.

The troops deployed into the forest in the pouring rain. I looked on from my attic window. At the edge of the forest they spread out. A long chain of them crept between the trees. Every pit, every bush, every hole was inspected. The soldiers even scanned the branches above so that they could see at once if the enemy were cunningly crouched there.

In the early evening the troops came back into the village again. Apparently they hadn't had any contact with the enemy, for they brought neither prisoners nor war wounded with them. Only the feet of twenty-four weary infantrymen were to be mourned: They had gotten blisters on their heels and toes from their ill-fitting, wet boots.

Herr Captain was enraged, and he took out his fury on my uncle. As mayor, he had to take it. After Herr Captain had poured four high-proof pear brandies down his throat for purposes of disinfection, he betrayed his secret commission to the mayor. The farmhands and the maids and I also learned the secret, because Herr Captain was sitting at the table in the kitchen with us.

With two more pear brandies, he divulged the entire maneuver strategy to us in his staccato military language. Maneuver orders. Wartime conditions. Enemy is a single person, a certain Robber Knapp. High-priority enemy, to be treated like a spy. Description: black hat. Disarm at once, or even better: shoot on sight.

It was soon no state secret to the rest of the community. A certain Grenadier Hudelmaier disclosed it in the Lion after five beers. Daniel had heard everything along with everyone else and he reported it to us straightaway.

It seems that about an hour after midday the soldiers had picked up an old woman. A monster of ugliness, very bent, with old, stinking clothes and a basket full of firewood on her back. Since they hadn't found a single other living soul in the forest, either friend or foe, this woman became an important person. Therefore Herr Captain insisted on conducting the interrogation himself, as the highest rank was always best at doing something like that. Did this dirty old wood woman know a certain Robber Knapp, Herr Captain asked, and had she seen any suspicious creatures in this forest now or earlier? And so forth. These were the questions that one learned as a royal officer—the sort of questions one used to ferret out a hidden enemy or spy. Apparently the old woman was not right in the head and she answered the questions about Robber Knapp a little strangely. Well, she knew a certain Plapp, the woman jabbered. Did he mean the one who was married to the second Kugler girl from Kaesbach, or was it Balthasar Plapp? Ah but he's been dead for the last eleven years—of quinsy, I think. Yes, and then there was also Isidor Plapp. If Herr General is looking for him he must look further, in Heilbronn. He was in prison there, because four years ago he had offended His Highness the King, Our Honorable Majesty, on the detour over the field sluice gate at Rappold. Otherwise she couldn't think of another Plapp, unless it should be that Herr General wasn't looking for Plapp but a Trapp. Then she knew one in Hinterbuechelberg and another in Sulzbach, but not in the closer Sulzbach but in the Sulzbach in the Limpurg district. She also knew a Trapp in—but the old woman was allowed to go no further. Herr Captain had put his hands to his head and ordered his sergeant to get the old bag out of his sight before he went just as crazy as she.

Grenadier Hudelmaier had been standing by and heard everything. He had requested permission to speak, because something struck him as strange. But Herr Captain was so excited that he bellowed at Grenadier Hudelmaier not to interfere in his superiors' deliberations and decision making. And besides, he would do well to leave the thinking to Herr Captain and the horses. So Grenadier Hudelmaier kept to himself what he was intending to report—namely, that the old woman with the basket on her back really had a very deep voice and was awfully unshaven under her head scarf.

The people in the pub had laughed so, said Daniel, and they'd bought Hudelmaier so many glasses of cider that he had to be carried home to his quarters afterward.

Old Daniel laughed so loudly while he was telling this that you could see his ribs bouncing up and down under his shirt. My uncle also let himself be infected, and his face twitched a little. But that was really quite a lot. I just didn't know why inwardly he was so pleased. Was he just glad because Herr Captain was taken in by Rober Knapp, or was he maybe a little bit pleased that Knapp hadn't been caught? I would have preferred the second!

For another whole day the soldiers combed through every possible hiding place in and around the village. They brought nothing out of the forest but a tremendous appetite, wet and dirty clothes, bloody toes, rubbed heels, and corns. The enemy was not to be conquered.

Then the company of the Crown Prince's Regiment marched back to Ludwigsburg, where they belonged.

The Truth Comes Out

CHRISTIAN WAS STILL NOT BACK.

Late in the morning I awakened with a hundred-pound weight of dreams on my chest. I was tired, and not even a salt stick tasted good. Of course Frederika noticed. She stroked my head. I liked her, and I made up my mind to tell her so sometime.

The entire day was worse than a waste. It should simply be stricken from memory. Nothing but rain! It was raining for the third day in a row, and the unripe hay was beginning to rot.

"Christian Knapp will be with his father in the robber's cave," said one of the under maids at supper. The other under maid said, "The poor mite is lying in the forest somewhere and is probably deathly ill. If he isn't dead already!"

My uncle was staring off into space very strangely.

"He's brooding too much!" whispered Frederika, and she

probably knew him the best. "But he really couldn't help it
that Christian ran away. Well, they shouldn't have taken the
Knapp children away from their mother! The only one to
blame for that is the schoolmaster, that devil! They say he
even said that people shouldn't be making such a fuss on
account of a robber's child. That people should be glad if
there's one less brat in the world."

It grew dark. Supper was over. Christian still hadn't
appeared.

"Perhaps he's already died of hunger!" said the young
hand. The only thing he ever thought of was food.

Then Daniel suggested that someone ask Frau Knapp if
perhaps Christian might be with his father. Certainly Frau
Knapp would be in touch with her husband.

Uncle paced back and forth in the mayor's office. His
heavy tread could be heard in the kitchen.

"Something's wrong with him," mused Frederika. "The
spirit of unrest is tormenting him." And then very softly she
added, "Or a bad conscience!"

The people in the village were also airing their opinions.

"The boy has taken off for America," our neighbor
Wheelwright Grau was supposed to have said. "I would have
done that at his age!"

"You and your America!" his old wife was said to have
scolded. "You aren't even brave enough to go out to the dung
heap at night!"

In any case, one thing was certain, the people in the village
said. The mayor hadn't managed to cope with the boy.

I was dog tired, but I kept on sitting there in the kitchen.

Frederika didn't mind. She knew that I had a heavy heart and could hardly sleep. The haying vacation wasn't over yet, and if the sun didn't come out tomorrow there wouldn't be any haying to do. Frederika let me stay in bed longer, and she also insisted I not try to hold a rake in my blistered hands.

If only Christian were back again!

Suddenly my uncle threw open the door. "You! Boniface! Run quickly down to the poorhouse, please, and ask Frau Knapp if she can come up here for a minute. I want to talk to her about something."

"Oh my!" said Frederika, and I grew red with surprise. Uncle had said *please*!

Frederika took off her apron. "I'll go with you," she said energetically. "The boy shouldn't run around alone at night. We might lose him again somehow!"

Frau Knapp prepared to come with us at once, as if she had been expecting it. I could see her tear-stained, sorrowful face in the light of the oil lamp.

"Does anyone know anything about Christian?" she asked in a trembling voice.

"Oh, God!" wailed Frederika, and I didn't trust myself to answer.

The heavens were dumping giant buckets of water onto Graab. Luckily the distance from the poorhouse to the mayor's house wasn't great.

My uncle was waiting in the doorway. He invited Frau Knapp into the kitchen, and I marveled at how friendly Uncle could be when he wasn't being the mayor. Still friendly, he asked Frau Knapp, "Have you heard anything from your son Christian?" He looked at her almost anxiously, as if he were afraid of the answer.

Frau Knapp seemed to have expected something else. Instead of answering she began to weep, and between sobs she stammered, "And I thought Christian was back again."

Hesitantly my uncle asked, "The people in the village say that Christian may possibly be with his father in the robber cave—that is, I mean, in the forest." There was a tiny bit of compassion in his voice. "And they also say," he continued, "that you have contact with the robber, I mean, with your husband. Can you possibly ask him whether Christian is safely stowed away there or whether—may God forbid—he is not?"

"That he is not!" sobbed Frau Knapp. "I just spoke with my husband two hours ago, and he knows nothing about Christian. He wouldn't have stood for it anyhow to have the boy live with him in the forest."

We all looked at one another, shocked.

"Well, where is he, then?" my uncle let slip, and Frederika added, "What a misfortune! Let nothing have happened to him!"

The lump of grief on my heart grew even heavier.

Frederika noticed it. "Is something the matter with you, boy?"

It was now or never. "Knapp isn't a robber at all!" I said as loudly as I could. "He didn't hold up the under ox drover and he never robbed Bofinger. I should know, after all!" This last was said boastfully.

Uncle looked up angrily. "What sort of foolishness are you talking there?" he barked at me.

I at once began to feel intimidated again by his harsh words. My heart sank right down to the soles of my feet. It was hard to get even one more word out. No! I wasn't going to be such a coward any longer!

"Knapp isn't a robber at all!" I repeated. "At the same time the under ox drover was being held up, Knapp was saving me from freezing to death. And he didn't rob Bofinger either. I know, because I saw and spoke with Knapp on the same evening and at the same time. Not in the Roth Valley, where the holdup was, but at the big, old oak in Devil's Ditch in the lake meadow."

Now it was out. It didn't matter what Uncle did to me. I ought to have said it much earlier anyhow!

You could have heard a fly cough in the kitchen. Only a piece of sapwood crackled in the stove.

Uncle pulled himself together first. He looked at me, utterly thunderstruck. He was probably considering how he would punish me. I feared the worst. I had spoken with the Robber Knapp behind his back! He would never forgive me. Still, I was glad I'd told him.

Frederika suddenly leapt up, ran to me, and took my head between her great hands, as if she had to protect me from powerful blows.

"You're really something, my Boniface!" she said, beaming, and then she challenged the mayor with her eyes.

He didn't say aye or nay, but he still looked thunderstruck. Then he stood up and went into his office.

A Sound in the Night

IN THE MIDDLE OF THE NIGHT I sat up in bed. The excitement of the evening and an inexplicable unease troubled me.

Uncle hadn't spoken a word to me, and Christian was still missing.

Some kind of a noise had awakened me. Certainly not the heavy rain, which pounded on the roof as if it wanted to drum it to pieces. The rain was actually rather soothing. It also wasn't a mouse. I knew mice well enough. I'd gotten used to them. They did gymnastics on the attic floor and in the rafters every night. Occasionally they tumbled onto the bedclothes and let out some gruesome mouse screams. Who knew what they did all night! But they couldn't disturb my sleep. Bats didn't keep me from sleeping, either. Occasionally one of those flying rats would lose its way and get into my room. Bats didn't make any noise—they whizzed like

shadows along the roof boards. And they were quite harmless. It wasn't true that they sucked the blood out of children
and old people. Something else must have awakened me.

It wasn't my hands, either. True, they were still burning. Frederika had smeared them with pinesap salve and
wrapped a strip of linen around each one. They were itching
a little, but Frederika had said that was a good sign, because
itching means healing.

The church tower clock struck three times—so it was just
midnight.

Someone was walking in the attic next door. I could hear
it quite clearly in spite of the rain. Who would be sneaking
around in the attic at midnight? Uncle? That wasn't his
heavy tread. Or Daniel, or the young hand, or one of the
maids? Absolutely not! Ten horses wouldn't drag them into
the attic at midnight. So, what, then? A ghost?

My scalp went cold. The blood must have gotten stuck in
my lower regions with fright! My toes were heavy with it.
Ghosts are lighter than air, I told myself. Therefore, what was
out in the attic could not be a ghost. The attic floorboards were
even creaking. But that didn't make me feel much better.

Frederika had recently told us that a murderer, some relative of the previous owner of the house, was supposed to
have been hanged in that very attic.

The ghost was at the door. The hinges turned in their cart
grease. A draft of air wafted past my face. So the door was
open already. I felt it. Someone was in the dark room with
me! For a moment my heart stopped. That was fear. I
wanted to yell, but I did something entirely different, some-

thing completely mindless. I pulled my head under my fat featherbed and rolled up like a hedgehog.

"Boniface!" whispered a trembling voice next to the bed. "Boniface! Don't yell! It's me!" A wet hand reached into the bed and touched me on the shoulder.

I jumped a mile. I was just gathering my strength to let out a yell that would be heard all over the house, when someone next to me said, "Don't yell! It's me. Christian Knapp."

Then I sat up in bed again. In front of me stood a dark form, not the hanged murderer but a trembling boy, Christian.

I was overjoyed. I grabbed the wet bundle and hugged him.

He was trembling and shivering, soaking wet, and frozen stiff.

"You'll catch your death!"

Christian's teeth were chattering.

"Take off your wet things, quick, and get into bed so I can warm you up! You're shivering like sour milk!"

Utterly exhausted, he fell into my bed. I hoped in the morning Frederika wouldn't think I was a bed wetter just because this frog soaked my bed. Christian was coughing like a consumptive. He needed a hot tea. I had to call Frederika. She would know what to do in a case like this.

First he had to quiet down. How could anyone be so unreasonable as to run around in horrible weather like this for three days! But never mind! I was just so glad that he was back again. Even if he was all wet and cold as an icicle.

He smelled strongly of the rain and the forest.

Soon his breathing grew quieter and he was coughing less

frequently. Was he already asleep? Gradually he stopped shivering. Just a little longer, then I'd go for Frederika.

Carefully I sneaked downstairs. I hoped the maid wouldn't be terrified when I appeared in her room so suddenly.

The door wasn't locked. Frederika was sound asleep. That came from all that work, and perhaps that was also why she was snoring so resoundingly.

"Frederika!" I said softly. "Don't be afraid! It's me, Boniface!"

Frederika quickly swallowed back two or three snores, and with it her sleep. Then she started up.

"What's the matter?" she said so forcefully that I was afraid she'd wake the whole house.

"It's me, Boniface!"

"Oh-god-oh-god-oh-god! Is something the matter with you, boy?"

"No, not me! But Christian's back. He's soaking wet, and I think he's caught his death. He's coughing like that consumptive Isidor Strauchberger. He needs a tea or something like that."

"He's come back? Well, thanks be to God! I'll come right away. Where is he?"

"In my bed."

"That's good!" Frederika put her apron on over her nightgown and went to the kitchen. There, she blew on the coals in the cookstove, laid kindling and a few ruffled pinecones on it, scooped water out of the bucket, took two lids off the stove top, and put the pot of water on the open fire. Beside the stove hung a linen bag filled with all kinds of dried herbs.

Frederika took a handful from the bag and sprinkled them in the pot of water. She waited until it came to a boil, let the witch's brew simmer for a while, strained off the leached-out herbs, and emptied the finished tea into a stoneware pot.

It didn't smell particularly good, this tea. Something between sweet clover and sauerkraut. I only hoped it would help!

We made our way up the stairs with the barn lantern. Christian was lying quietly in bed. His breathing was slow and strong.

Frederika put the teapot on the floor and felt his forehead. "Well, good, he's certainly still alive! He's a healthy fellow. He can take a lot." Although she knew the boy couldn't hear her, she fussed over him; "Christian! Oh, Christian! Whatever have you been up to?" Then she shook him gently. "Drink, Christian! This tea will bring the dead to life. Wake up! You must drink the tea while it's hot or it will only do you half as much good."

Christian was surprised to see Frederika standing there in the room.

"Don't worry, I won't tell on you." The maid waited until Christian had drunk the tea. Then she took his dripping trousers and shirt. "I'll try to find something dry for him. I'll look in on you both early tomorrow." She took the barn lantern and went back downstairs.

I slipped into bed.

Christian opened his eyes once more. He moved over to the side so that I had enough room. Before I was completely asleep, I had the thought that Christian and I were breathing in exactly the same rhythm. As if the two of us shared one breath.

A Kiss on the Cheek

CHRISTIAN KNAPP WAS BACK AGAIN, and the bad weather was gone. The rain stopped drumming on our roof. Out the window, a wonderful morning greeted us. That was a good sign.

I hurried into my shirt and trousers and ran down to the kitchen. Frederika was already busy with pots and pans again. She was in a good mood and was doing her usual singing up and down the scale. Only today the notes were much stronger and the scale was longer, and every now and again Frederika would jump several notes at a time. A respectable fire was burning in the stove, and the kitchen smelled of apple wood and malt coffee.

How lucky that there was a Frederika!

She broke off her scales and asked me about Christian.

"He's sleeping like a bear."

"That's good! He surely has a lot of sleep to catch up on. I'll go look in on him shortly."

"Where's my uncle?" I asked.

The maid pointed to the mayor's office door with her ladle.

"Frederika," I said, "now I need all your fingers!"

"What do you want with my fingers?" she asked.

"You have to cross them hard now."

I went to the door of the mayor's office.

Frederika was shocked. "Boy! What are you doing? You aren't thinking of going in there?"

"Yes," I said. "Today I have to. I have to get something straightened out."

Frederika grew very pale. She sighed like a startled brown owl, put her ladle down on the kitchen table, and quickly crossed her fingers on both hands.

My knock was acknowledged with a surprised "Yes?" on the other side of the door.

"Good morning, Uncle!"

Once more, incredulity and astonishment. "Oh, it's you, Boniface! Yes, what do you want so early in the morning?"

"I need to speak with Your Honor!"

My uncle was surprised. His faced showed wonder. But only very briefly. Then his impenetrable mayor's face dropped into place. No sign of either rejection or favor. "So, you want to speak with me!"

Oh dear! He drew his eyebrows together. Pincers closed around my heart. I gathered all my courage.

"Yes, I must speak with Your Honor."

My uncle winked. The threatening eyebrows moved apart, and the crease between them was gone.

"Then speak!" he said, firmly but gently.

"Christian is back!"

Now it was out.

"I know!"

So he knew it already. Probably Frederika had blabbed.

"Your Honor knows already?"

"Yes, he came in last night. It was impossible not to hear him."

Now I was surprised by the surprise. What should I say to that? Uncle always knew everything. He probably heard the grass growing too.

But then came the hard thing, the hardest. He would never forgive me for violating his prohibition against Christian.

"But . . . Christian," I said. "He's with me in my room! He's sleeping in my bed!" I stammered, half fearfully, half bravely.

Uncle looked inside my head. He probably saw everything in there: my fear, my courage, and everything else.

"Yes, of course, where else should he be sleeping? The young hand wouldn't have let him in," said Uncle. Nothing else.

I hadn't expected that from this stern man. All of a sudden the joy so flooded over me that I forgot all my good manners in a moment and gave Uncle a kiss on the cheek. Afterwards I was shocked at myself, as was Uncle too.

In the kitchen a pan or a stove lid fell clattering to the flag-stone floor.

"Oh, that Frederika!" said Uncle, and as he said it he laughed lightheartedly, as we laugh when there is no little spot tarnishing our souls.

The Sun Returns

THE SUN WAS MAKING UP for all that it had neglected in the past few days. You would almost have thought that it had nothing else in mind but to save the hay and make usable fodder out of the muddy grass. Farmers and hands, maids and day workers, and all the children who could hold a rake turned the damp stuff this way and that. The sun's rays poured down on it so that it steamed. The moldy smell grew ever less, and by noon some blades were already crunching under the rakes. God be thanked! It wasn't too late after all. If it got this hot again tomorrow, the hay could be brought in by late afternoon.

Uncle stood beside me under the pear tree. I had to tell him everything very precisely. How and when I had met Robber Knapp, how it had come about, and what I had seen and heard there.

The maids and men looked over at us curiously. They

would have loved to know what Uncle and I were talking about. I heard the young hand at the lower end of the field: "He doesn't even have to work, this dandy from the city. No, of course not. How could a person with such delicate little hands be expected to work?" He was certainly talking about me. I would so very much have liked to be able to work.

My uncle turned toward the young hand. So he'd heard something too. I was ashamed of my stupid, good-for-nothing hands.

"Enough of that foolish chatter now!" chided Uncle, and probably even the hand realized that he had reached the limit of the mayor's patience. In any case, he held his flapping jaw.

In spite of my bandaged hands I again turned the hay for Uncle.

Christian came. As if nothing had happened, he took up his rake beside Chief Hand Daniel and tossed the hay from one side to the other. The servants' mouths dropped in surprise. However, the really strange thing was that the mayor kept on working as if everything were all very normal.

The older under maid couldn't stand it any longer. Did the mayor not see, or didn't he want to see?

The maid took a few steps forward and called across half a meadow, "Mayor! Christian Knapp is here! He's back again!" Then she waited curiously.

My uncle turned to her. "Of course he's here. Where else would he be?" And then he laughed. But I was the only one who heard it because the others were all too far away.

The Insurrection

THE NEXT DAY the hay was brought in. On the whole, the farmers seemed content. It could have turned out much worse. The hay didn't smell particularly good after so much rain, but the cattle would eat it. They had to, there wasn't any other. It was hoped that the oehmd would be better.

The haying vacation was over now and Schoolmaster Altmayer had to be endured again. I had great difficulty with him because I hated him like the plague. I could no longer keep a normal face whenever he came near me. My anger wouldn't stay concealed. The schoolmaster was irritated today. Not only were we repugnant to him, but he couldn't stand himself.

Two hours had gone by, the times tables and stories of the Apostles. Now came memorization drill. What else? Probably the schoolmaster himself didn't know anything more.

The sayings were already through the first row. Then out in the back there was some kind of a sound. What it was exactly couldn't be established afterwards.

The schoolmaster turned fiery red. "Who committed that indecency?"

Of course no one answered. Who would volunteer for hell?

I could have sworn it wasn't a fart.

Altmayer asked once again, and his voice shot from low to high: "Who committed that indecency?"

My anger grew. What did the man want? It wasn't anything at all!

Altmayer considered for a moment. And as usual he savored our fear.

"Christian Knapp!" he called after a long moment. "It was you! Come up here!"

"No!" cried Christian in mortal fear. "It wasn't me! It wasn't anyone!"

The schoolmaster stiffened. He turned red, then white, then he trembled, and he did something that no one had ever seen him do before. He jumped up and climbed over the benches to the back, grabbed Christian Knapp, dragged him to the teacher's desk, pulled down Christian's trousers, and hit him on the naked behind with his stick. In front of all the girls.

That was too much. Even a schoolmaster wasn't allowed to do that. "Stop!" I cried to the front of the room, and I was surprised that I wasn't peeing in my pants with fear. "Stop! You aren't allowed to do that!"

Altmayer started, and now something else happened that was equally unexpected.

The other boys and girls banged their fists on the benches, and the entire upper class called and bellowed and cried: "You aren't allowed to do that! You aren't allowed to do that! You aren't allowed to do that!" And the fists kept time to it.

Beanpole leapt to the front of the room and placed himself between the schoolmaster and Knapp. Beanpole was almost a head taller, so he didn't need to say anything. He only opened his mouth a little, and the entire upper class could see and hear his gigantic tusks of teeth grinding with anger.

Then suddenly it was still in the upper class. Even time stood still.

What had we done?

We had destroyed order in the school.

And I had started it.

But I didn't regret it, not one little bit.

The door opened, the assistant teacher from the lower class rushed in, saw the wax-pale, swaying schoolmaster, and led him safely out.

Two Lambs

ON OUR WAY HOME the Devil's cat reappeared. It ran across the street from left to right. Left to right—that had to mean something bad!

The catastrophe couldn't be avoided. I'd probably have to go to the orphanage. Uncle would send me away.

He would already have heard of my rebellion in school. News like that traveled fast in Graab. And I was the ringleader! He wouldn't let me get away with that. I had rebelled against authority. Even the schoolmaster was authority. He was installed by the consistory, which was appointed by the king. So I hadn't just shown disrespect to the schoolmaster, but also to the king. And it was worse still if you looked at the situation carefully—and such things must be looked at carefully. For the king was installed by the will of God. So I had insulted God!

Never had I been so anxious before the midday meal.

We were sad, Christian and I. Things had been going so well for us in the mayor's house. Where in the world would there be another woman like Frederika? So uncommonly good! We liked her. I most of all. Uncle was almost like a father to me. A stern father, naturally, but I much preferred that. What would I want with a father who didn't know what he wanted? Or with one who was dumber than his children?

We were all sitting around the table, and everything seemed normal. Uncle wasn't acting any differently than usual. He asked Christian and me if we wanted to take a little hike up to the high field after dinner. There were two lambs up there that needed to be brought down. But we shouldn't think of it as child's play. Those little beasts could often be quite stubborn, and they could be a lot of trouble to manage.

Of course we wanted to go get the lambs.

So disaster wasn't so close yet. Perhaps the talk of my crime hadn't reached the mayor's house yet. But it would soon. The amazing thing was that Schoolmaster Altmayer hadn't paid a visit to my uncle himself. To be sure, Frederika was looking at me a little strangely. So I thought. But I could have been mistaken too. She didn't look angry.

We walked up to the high field and got the two little lambs. It turned out to be hard work. The baby sheep were not only stubborn, they jumped foolishly about and always wanted to do exactly what we didn't want them to do. Nevertheless, it was a wonderful time, and it would have been even more wonderful if I weren't going to have to leave it all. We intended to ask Uncle if we could take care of the lambs all by ourselves. At least until I had to go to the orphanage.

Christian remarked that I shouldn't have scolded the schoolmaster. Then everything would have stayed the way it used to be. He would, of course, have received his blows, but that would have been bearable.

"No!" I said. "I don't regret it, not in the least! The schoolmaster goes way overboard and has for a long time, and he's not allowed to. Somebody had to tell him."

Christian sighed and ran his hand over my head. "Say," he said, "your hair's getting long again. You look much better this way than with the shorn-sheep cut."

"You have a shorn-sheep cut yourself!"

"Sure, but it's not the same thing for me."

The evening meal was normal. Uncle was normal. Frederika and the other maids were normal. And the young hand ate and ate. That was normal too.

Cautiously I began to feel happy again, but not so much that the disappointment afterwards would be too great. I wanted to try out my uncle, and so I asked him about the lambs and feeding them. Yes, he'd thought exactly the same thing. Christian and I should each have our own lamb, and of course each of us should take care of it all by himself. "But woe to you if either of them is neglected. A lamb is God's creature!" said Uncle with almost ceremonial seriousness.

Ah, how beautiful the world was! If only time could stand still. That would keep the disaster outside the house.

And then—oh, horror—it arrived!

Beadle and Police Constable Fuenfkorn reported back from his errand. He had advised all the members of the church convention to report to the mayor's house tonight, with one exception. The schoolmaster was indisposed and begged to be excused.

"What does *indisposed* mean? Is he really sick or not?" The mayor was annoyed. "It's about him in the first place. Does he want to dodge it?"

"With your permission, sir. Don't know. He wasn't in bed. He was packing up his household. I think he's planning to take a trip. *Exakt!*"

"Oho, aha!"

So disaster hadn't struck yet—though it was coming soon. Tonight the church convention was meeting. They were the very people who could decide my future. Orphanage or not.

I went out to the barn again. Christian was lying beside his lamb in the straw, head to head, and they were butting each other in fun. I took my little lamb in my arms. I think it already liked me, for it licked my hands.

"Oh, Boniface," said Christian with a sigh. "How nice the world can be!"

"Oh, yes!" I answered. Nothing better occurred to me to say, and then Christian said, "It's enough to make you cry!" And then, "We're going to stink of sheep!"

We were in complete agreement there too.

Later we were lying in bed and couldn't get to sleep, although we were dog tired.

The church convention was meeting down in the mayor's office. We recognized each of the voices below. Beadle and Police Constable Fuenfkorn was standing watch at the front door, and he made sure that no one who hadn't been invited disturbed this important secret meeting.

I was very agitated. It was, after all, about me. I wanted to listen, but Christian said that that was something you don't do—and besides, we'd learn our fate soon enough. And there he was most certainly right.

Then Christian fell asleep. He was breathing quietly and regularly, and that was proof that he wasn't dreaming about anything terrible.

Oh God! Thank you for creating Christian, even if it was on a detour by way of a robber!

The Orphanage

WHAT A MORNING! It shone in through the window, sunny, friendly, and demanding activity.

Christian was already awake. Propped up on his elbows, he was waiting for me to open my eyes. That's the way it looked, anyway. He said, "You slept well, anyhow."

"What do you mean 'anyhow'?"

Then it all came back to me: the schoolmaster, the church convention, the orphanage. The decision had certainly been made by now.

The house was peaceful, as usual. The usual sounds were coming from the kitchen. Frederika was banging her pots and pans. A couple of cows were mooing in the barn next door. They probably wanted someone to come and milk them.

There were only gloomy thoughts lurking in my head.

"I'm going to lie here and wait until Uncle or someone comes to get me."

"That's wrong!" said Christian. "We should go ask Frederika. She'll be sure to know what the church convention decided last night. She'll tell us. She's always on our side. If you have to go to the orphanage, we'll just run away. So it's important for us to know in advance what's going to happen. That way we can ship out to America."

"You're crazy!"

"Would you rather go to the orphanage?"

"Of course not!"

"Well, then, come on. Let's go ask her."

Frederika was alone in the kitchen. Breakfast was over. Daniel was bringing the manure out of the barn with a wheelbarrow. I heard the older under maid singing in there with the cows, loud and off-key. You couldn't get any more off-key.

"Where've you been? You sleepyheads!" Frederika fussed. "How can anyone be so lazy? God created this beautiful day for you too. But you must certainly have already known that there's no school today. Nevertheless there's plenty of work for you. Or have you already forgotten your lambs? And the chicken coop needs tending. There's so much manure in there now, pretty soon the hens won't even be able to get inside."

There was milk and bread and butter.

"What's the matter with you?" Frederika asked. "You look as if the hens stole your bread."

"Frederika . . ." I asked carefully and daringly, "what was so important that they held a meeting of the church convention yesterday?"

"Well, you aren't exactly what I'd call curious! But it's not much of a secret. The whole village probably knows already. The schoolmaster is leaving. He's going today. He even intends to sell his house."

"Why? Not because of me?"

"Joker!" said Frederika with a laugh. "Certainly not because of you. There are more important people than you. They say the schoolmaster committed an indecency. It's a terrible disgrace for the schoolmaster, since he was always such an upright and respectable man."

"What kind of indecency?"

"That's not for you to be concerned with, Boniface."

"And what about me, Frederika? The orphanage—do I have to go now?"

"Boy, don't you like it here with us? Why would you ever want to go to the orphanage? Don't do that to me!" Frederika grabbed me and pressed me so hard to her cushiony breast that I could scarcely breathe anymore.

"No, I don't want to at all!" I panted when she released me.

And many heavy stones tumbled from my heart.

I put my arms around Frederika's neck, pulled her head down to me, and gave her a big, loving kiss.

Herr Gaunt

TWO STRANGERS ARRIVED in the village at about the same time. The first was our new schoolmaster; the other was bad news.

The schoolmaster was moderately young; the stranger was ageless, and he looked like a good-for-nothing, like a gendarme without a uniform.

Each spent almost an hour with my uncle in the mayor's office. That Uncle should meet for so long with the schoolmaster was understandable, for they had a great many things to discuss. The recent difficulties with Altmayer, for example, and the awful conditions in our school. But why Uncle should waste an hour of his time with the other one was inexplicable. Such good-for-nothings can be scented from far off, even against the wind. Why didn't my uncle smell anything wrong? They said the good-for-nothing was lodging at the Lion for a few days. We'd see what came of that! Anything could be believed of such people, but nothing respectable. What did my uncle have to do with such a low person?

The day the new schoolmaster taught the upper class for the first time, we couldn't get over our wonderment. At first I thought, this schoolmaster is a crackpot: He's only trying to test us or trap us with some rotten, devilish trick. No teacher just throws the stick into the wastebasket as if it didn't matter at all. What will he use to knock sense into the brutes and the lazybones? His bare hand? No teacher lets the stick out of his hand. Even in the Latin School the stick saw use, though not much. There's no such thing as a school without beating. It would be too perfect.

Then he said that he didn't wish to be called Herr Schoolmaster, because his name wasn't "Schoolmaster" but "Gaunt." Gaunt, like the opposite of fat. That was funny, but I didn't dare laugh. Only a few hard-boiled characters took a risk, and their mouths twitched a little.

That surprised the new schoolmaster and he asked if people in Graab didn't know how to laugh. At which we were again astonished and looked at each other dumbly.

Herr Gaunt's face took on a grave, sad expression. "Well," he said to himself, but loud enough so that we could hear, "that will come."

I already knew by this time that I liked him. Of course, he was no ordinary teacher. He talked with us perfectly normally, like Frederika, or Christian, or Uncle when he wasn't being mayor. Not like former Herr Schoolmaster Altmayer, and not like the minister when he was standing between heaven and earth in the pulpit. He talked with us as we would like all people to talk with us.

Herr Gaunt said that he came from the Hohenloh region, from Mergentheim, and he asked if anyone knew this beautiful city. Of course we shook our heads. How should any of us know Mergentheim? It was very far away, perhaps as far as Cannstatt. The schoolmaster talked for an hour about his hometown. He described the city so beautifully and so well that we believed that it must be in the Promised Land, or pretty close to it. A stupid housefly was banging against a window. Its buzzing disturbed us. It was so quiet. We were in another world.

Recess was already past and no one noticed. We couldn't get over our amazement.

It got to be noon, and weren't even glad about it. It was so wonderful in school.

"Until tomorrow," said the schoolmaster when he dismissed us, and it occurred to me that we had forgotten to thank God, the king, and the schoolmaster for the benefits received. And this day we ought to have at least thanked the schoolmaster!

A Fresh Wind

BY AFTERNOON the new teacher was already the talk of the village. Wherever I went they were talking about him, maligning him, complaining about him.

How could he be any good? Without a stick! He'd thrown it into the wastebasket in front of the children! He had discarded the regulations! Who was going to have any respect for a teacher without a stick? He was going to ruin the school!

That evening the local school board was convened, and because it was so important, the village council came too, and the citizens' committee, and the church convention. The mayor's office was completely full, and only half of them were inside. The door was left open and the remainder settled in the kitchen. The many men were sweaty, and it was smelly. There was a need for more air. Open the windows! No, that wouldn't do! Then the whole village could hear. So all the windows were shut, all the doors opened, and only the front door was closed.

We—Christian and I—left the door to our garret open, lay in bed, and heard everything coming up the staircase. Therefore I can report exactly what all the village bigwigs threw up to the new schoolmaster and what the schoolmaster preached to the village bigwigs.

They were waiting only for the minister. He could indulge himself in coming a little late. He was the only one who didn't have to pay a ten-kreuzer penalty for it.

"I'll show the little schoolmaster the ropes," said Strauchberger to everyone from the local school board, and he said it so often that no one paid any attention to him anymore.

"What does this young pup think, anyway? He comes strolling in here yesterday and today he already wants to turn the whole place upside down!" said Sawmiller Bay.

Ludwig Raith of the citizens' committee had to add his two cents. "I was thrashed by the schoolmaster in the old days for seven long years. Why should it be any different for my sons? That's the way it's supposed to be!"

The minister arrived.

"Why are you so late?" Uncle reproved him. He was the only man in the village who spoke so familiarly to the minister.

Christian whispered to me, "Now they can get going! Let's cross our fingers for the schoolmaster!"

At first the village bigwigs let loose with their complaints. The business with the stick in the wastebasket—the schoolmaster ought not to have done that. And the children must, of course, address him as "Herr Schoolmaster" in the future. And there was no reason at all to discontinue the memorization drill. What could serve a person better in life than the wise sayings out of the book of aphorisms? And so on. And what good will it do if he describes the world to the children as being so beautiful? Nobody will want to stay in the village anymore!

The minister said, "It is, of course, not necessarily a tragedy if a fresh wind blows through the village. But the wind must not be so strong that it demolishes everything. Still, we must ask ourselves if it is properly within a schoolmaster's purview to create a wind."

Whereupon a few councilors laughed because they thought of wind as something impolite.

My uncle asked the schoolmaster how he saw the situation and what surprises he still had up his sleeve.

Then the schoolmaster spoke. Loudly and clearly, for he had to be heard not only in the mayor's office but also in the kitchen and the corridor.

Christian held his fingers in front of my nose, and I understood him immediately. Now we had better cross all our fingers, for the schoolmaster's fate was about to be decided.

At the beginning now and then one or another of the village bigwigs would throw in a "Hey, now!" or a "Listen here!" but these interjections became fewer and fewer, and then only our schoolmaster was speaking. We could uncross our fingers. There was no more danger.

And what did the schoolmaster say? The large classes had to be divided, since there wasn't classroom space that was decent or sufficient. He was convinced that the terrible crowding and the unhygienic conditions had caused the grisly scarlet fever epidemic some years before. And because a few village bigwigs had to ask what *unhygienic* meant, he gave them a brief lecture on cleanliness.

"How smart our schoolmaster is!" Christian whispered to me.

Moreover, he insisted he would not hit the children. That was not only unmanly, but it was unpedagogic. He immediately explained the word *pedagogic*, so that no one had to ask what *that* was supposed to be.

It was very quiet in the mayor's house. Except for the schoolmaster, no one else said a word. Christian had drifted off into a sound sleep, like a man content with himself and the world. So I had to keep to myself what I wanted to say to him. Which was that I thought the village bigwigs had learned more tonight than in all the seven years of their schooling and in the additional three years of Sunday School.

KAROLYN

TIME ROLLED ON, uninterrupted and without regard for
human beings and their affairs, important and unimportant.

The new schoolmaster had been in Graab for quite a
while now. We'd gotten used to him so quickly that no one
ever thought about Altmayer anymore.

The upper class had been divided into two smaller classes.
One met in the morning, the other in the afternoon. Thank
goodness I was still with Christian and his sister Karolyn.
Also the great Beanpole was with us, and I was glad about
that. He didn't bother me anymore. Recently he'd even
asked me if I would go fishing with him, since he knew there
were a few big trout in the Roth. Of course I couldn't do that,
because my uncle was mayor. Even if I was only his nephew,
I still mustn't steal the king's trout.

The schoolmaster had turned the whole school upside
down. He never made any cleanliness inspections.

"Why should I have you show me a little piece of cloth that is only there for show? The handkerchiefs you really use are dirty and spotted, and those are the ones where the bacteria and bacilli are lurking. And these invisible little creatures are what make us ill. It's more important," he said, "for everyone to know how important cleanliness is for health."

Not once did we ever have to memorize pious sayings. After a few days the boys and girls of Graab knew that in addition to the Holy Land and the kingdom of Wuerttemburg and America—to which some Graabers had emigrated—there were many other countries in the world. All that wasn't so new to me. I'd already heard of them in the Latin School in Cannstatt.

On this particular day, Karolyn was absent. Was she sick?

During the first recess I asked Christian. He didn't know either. He suspected that mean old Gayer wouldn't let her come to school because there was too much work to be done at home. I hoped nothing had happened to her. I was anxious to find out.

Recently I'd overheard a conversation between our two under maids. I'd been terribly shocked at what they were saying. Gayer was supposedly carrying on with his maid. "And just picture this," one said to the other, "now Gayer's going to let her go. They say he's afraid of the gossip in the village and so he wants 'this sluttish little beast' out of his house. On account of the public morals in the village."

Who knew what a person like that would do to Karolyn? Gayer was capable of anything.

After lunch we worked together, Christian and I. The

daily chores had to be done: the lambs cared for, the chickens fed, wood carried into the kitchen, the chicken coop cleaned, water replaced in the toilet, the bucket in the kitchen filled, and whatever else there was to be done in a farmyard.

Finally we were going along the old church path to Schoenbronn, between meadows and fields of spelt and oats. The sun was beautiful and hot. We could cool off in the lake. I would really love to swim again.

"Can you swim? Like a duck or a goose?" asked Christian.

"Not that well, but I did get across the Neckar!"

"Afterwards, once we know what's going on with Karolyn, show me!"

There were whole bunches of bellflowers in the Frankish meadow. I was happy that Christian noticed the flowers. Most of the village boys never noticed anything like that. For them the only thing that was important was whether the cows ate their feed or not. They found a particularly nice tree beautiful only because it meant many cords of wood. And which of the village boys noticed the curious eyes of a calf? The udder was important, for from it came either a great deal of milk or little.

At the tree meadow in front of Abel's Cliff we turned off to the Gayer farm. A woodpecker hammered unconcerned on an old pear tree stump.

We crept once around the farmyard. The Gayer dog started barking. "He's just as vicious and sneaky as Gayer," said Christian. "It's lucky he's chained!"

We lay down in the meadow within hearing distance

of the dog. We took turns watching the door of the house and the property over the edge of the grass. At some point Karolyn would have to show herself, if she wasn't sick.

The warmth made me sleepy. The humming and whirring and buzzing of every possible fly, bee, dragonfly, hornet, and other flying odds and ends filled my ears. The honey-sweet fragrance of clover and a mixture of other flower and grass scents filled my nose.

My eyes closed.

I must have slept a good while. The sun was already quite low over the mountains. Christian was tickling my nose with a blade of grass. "We have to go home," he said. "Your uncle gets crabby if we come late for supper."

"And Karolyn?"

"Nothing heard and nothing seen!"

"Shall I go up to the house and ask?"

"Gayer will throw you right out backwards!"

"But we have to know what's going on with Karolyn."

A peacock butterfly fluttered over us to a blue-violet meadow sage.

"We'll wait a little longer."

"We can run back really fast afterwards."

The Graab church clock struck in the distance. "Was that eight or nine times?"

"I think eight."

"Then we still have a little time."

A door in the Gayer house closed with a bang. Now someone had come out.

I almost cried aloud with joy. It was Karolyn. She was going to the village well with two buckets. Quickly we ran in an arc around the Gayer farm to the village well.

"Karolyn!"

"Oh God! It's you and Boniface!"

"What's the matter? Why weren't you in school today?"

"I had to work."

"That's a rotten trick! Gayer's not allowed to do that. He has to send you to school."

"Don't get excited, Boniface!" said Christian softly. "You see how it is. Gayer can do whatever he wants."

"I'll tell my uncle."

"Oh, leave it! The main thing is, nothing's wrong with my sister."

How pretty Karolyn was! She had nice ears and a nose that wasn't too big, too small, too fat, or too measly. Her rose-hip-pink mouth was exactly where it belonged, down to a hairsbreadth. Yes, and her sad-happy eyes! Really, I liked them the best. When she looked at me, I was no longer myself. Then I couldn't think straight, and I was both sad and happy at the same time.

Christian had the same eyes. I liked him for that too.

"Have you been listening at all?" asked Christian. "Karolyn just said that Gayer always goes away in the evenings and comes home late. So we can meet again in the evenings when he's away. Then we'll have more time."

"Yes, maybe the day after tomorrow, on Saturday. Then it won't matter if it gets to be a little later."

"I have to go now. Gayer scolds really foul-mouthed if I stay out too long," said Karolyn.

"All right, then. Saturday!" said Christian. "When it's completely dark, I'll give a tawny owl's call three times. We'll be right by the little frog pond behind the Gayer farm."

"Be careful, you two!"

"You too!"

The Rendezvous

SATURDAY. The night was unsettled. The weather didn't know what it wanted to do. There were masses of clouds, but every now and then a ragged piece would tear away and the moon would shine through, like a meager little lamp through a hole.

Right after supper we walked to Schoenbronn. Night was only half as threatening with two of us. Thank God we didn't have to cross Devil's Ditch. Christian only went there when he knew his father was waiting for him. Next to his father, the Devil or any spooks like that were only pindling little fellows.

Fireflies flickered like ghost eyes all around us. When I grabbed for one, the light was gone, and my hand was empty.

There was croaking in the little frog pond. The frogs were what gave it its name. So we weren't even startled when one of the little creatures plopped into the pond in front of us.

A steamy, warm draft rose from the water. We sat down under the twisted pine. I'd have liked to dangle my feet in the warm water, but I was afraid that something would grab me by the toes and pull me in. I'd show the invisible monster! I'd pee on it.

Christian saw me and whispered, "Anyone can hear that miles away, and besides, you aren't supposed to do that. Anyone who pees in the water is peeing in God's face. That's what they say," said Christian. Then he gave the tawny owl's call three times. He did it so well that I was really startled, because it made me think there was one sitting right next to me.

We listened to the night. A breeze made the pine needles tremble.

"Where's Karolyn?" I whispered into Christian's ear.

"We have to be patient. She can't just go out whenever she feels like it."

Some kind of monster was swimming around in the water. Perhaps it was just a frog or a snake or a muskrat. You can't tell very clearly at night. All that was audible was the sound of the furrow it made in the water. I drew my feet back.

Steps were approaching from Schoenbronn. Thank God, Karolyn was coming!

"Here we are!" I was about to call, but Christian held my mouth closed. "That's not Karolyn," he whispered. "She doesn't have a heavy stride like that."

Had Gayer discovered us?

I went to stand up. Perhaps I wanted to run away. Christian held on to me. "Sit quietly," he breathed in my ear.

Still a few more careful steps toward us, then we heard nothing more. The man, if it was one, must be very close to us.

For a long time, nothing. It was hard for me to sit without moving like that. Both my buttocks hurt.

Gayer's door opened and shut. It needed oiling, it squeaked horribly. I hoped it wasn't Karolyn. She would walk right into the arms of the stranger.

No, it must be Gayer himself. He left quite normally along the church path to Graab. His steps were clearly audible.

Suddenly the other man was beside us. This was it!

No, he probably didn't even see us. He went quickly along behind Gayer on the church path in the direction of Graab.

Quite a bit later Karolyn came out. "Gayer was suspicious," she reported. "As if he knew what I was planning. But then he left anyway."

We sat for a long time under the pine by the frog pond. We puzzled back and forth. Who was the man who had waited for Gayer and then followed him on the path to Graab? What did he want with him? The clouds thinned. The moon shone down on us more brightly. I saw Karolyn sitting beside me. Only briefly, then massive clouds moved between us again. A favorable breeze carried a few incomplete clock strikes toward us from the church tower. Otherwise I had no idea of how time was passing. As far as I was concerned it could have stood still. At least as long as I was sitting between Christian and Karolyn.

Mysterious Business

AFTER MIDDAY DINNER the strange man was again with Uncle in the mayor's office.

If I'd been the mayor, I wouldn't have let this unpleasant man take one step over the mayoral threshold.

Uncle called me in. Oh, horror! What had I done? And what did I have to do with this strange man?

He was sitting there, brazenly, opposite my uncle.

"Sit down!" commanded Uncle. He was the mayor once more, and therefore I needn't be surprised that the conversation that followed was official through and through.

He was looking me steadily in the face. I could do that too. I forced myself not to blink one single time.

The strange, unpleasant man asked my uncle, "Can he be relied on?"

"He can," he answered, and then to me he said, "Boniface, pay close attention!"

Uncle was being very mysterious.

"Nothing that you hear in this room is anybody else's business. Do you understand me? This is so secret, at least for now, that you mustn't breathe a word of it. The man opposite me is a secret policeman. He's investigating the holdups in our district. That's why he's here."

A light went on in my head.

The secret policeman fixed his gaze on me. "You're clever enough to understand all of this, aren't you?" he said in a gravelly voice.

Still, I couldn't stand him, no matter how important or how good a secret policeman he might be. "Yes!" I said, more to my uncle. "Yes, I think I'll understand it."

"Well, then, listen! The investigation into the case of the holdups promises to be quite successful. I'll say no more about that to you. It doesn't even concern you. Now, first of all, I want you to tell me exactly what happened to you on the eighteenth of March, the night you got lost in the forest. Then you must tell me about the fifth of May. Allegedly you saw Robber Knapp, and allegedly he even spoke with you. Do you understand my questions?"

"Yes!"

I told the secret policeman the story of the man with the black hat, and I didn't fail to add that it was also possible that I dreamed it all. I wasn't sure. But what happened on the fifth of May was an entirely different story. I'd just experienced that recently, and I was sure that I hadn't dreamed that time. I told him everything that I heard and saw.

"You know that someday you will roast horribly in hell if

this isn't true? And you'll be imprisoned there for at least a lifetime!"

"I know!"

"And one thing more," pronounced the secret policeman in his gravelly voice. "I don't want to see you and the other children loitering around the Gayer house in Schoenbronn anymore. Not by day and not by night! Do you understand? That's an order!"

And my uncle added somewhat more calmly and amiably, "Stay away from that house in the near future. I can't tell you why, but it has nothing to do with you. And furthermore— not a word to Christian, not even to Frederika!"

"Yes!" I said, and I thought: Aha! So something's going on at the Gayer house! But, naturally, I didn't dare ask. And the unknown person we heard near Gayer's last Saturday— it was this man himself. Of course! Everything came together now.

"You can go," said Uncle. "And not a word to anyone at all!"

The Robber Is Caught!

THE SCISSORS GRINDER was there in the yard.

Frederika had also brought in the big scissors. I was familiar with those already. As soon as I saw them I thought at once of my hair. Uncle had certainly noticed that it had grown back quite a lot.

And then it happened. Just as the big shears were being sharpened on the stone wheel, with the sparks flying, Uncle came along.

He watched for a while. Perhaps to see if the grinder was doing a good job. Then he looked at me and at Frederika. Now it was all clear to me—the scissors, my head, and Frederika. I was going to be shorn like a lamb again!

Naturally Frederika noticed too. She awaited the orders of her master, and as always she looked directly into my heart. She was torn this way and that way, but there was no way out of it. She knew it, and I knew it too.

The scissors were sharpened. Frederika looked at me pityingly, and even I realized that it would be wisest if we just got it over with. Why annoy and irritate Uncle? I went into the kitchen and sat on the stool. That way Frederika could easily go around my head with the scissors. Then Uncle came in. Wouldn't he be satisfied to see that we were obeying him of our own accord, without him having to criticize and create a fuss first?

"What are you doing there?" he asked quietly.

"Oh well," said Frederika, "we know, of course, that it's high time for a haircut. And so we thought we'd do it now, voluntarily. I was just about to shear Boniface."

"But, Frederika," objected Uncle, "let his hair grow a little more. I don't want you to treat him like a sheep." He went to the office door, and before we could close our mouths, which had fallen open in sheer astonishment, Uncle turned once more and said firmly, "Just make sure he doesn't get any lice!"

Moments later, the secret policeman returned. He hurried into the mayor's office, and scarcely two or three minutes later he stormed out with Uncle. Without taking the least notice of us, they left the house.

"Something's going on," said Frederika, and she combed through my hair again.

"Frederika," I said, "stop combing! I want to see where the two of them are going!"

When I jumped down, I could see nothing more of them, and so I couldn't even find out what direction they hurried off in.

Oh, please, just not that! I was convinced that the secret policeman had located Knapp, and now the two of them had gone to get him. Or were they intending something entirely different?

In the early evening not only the two came back, but four! The secret policeman and my uncle must have bumped into Beadle and Police Constable Fuenfkorn somewhere, for he was with them too. But the fourth wasn't Knapp. Thanks be to God, they hadn't caught him. The fourth was Gayer. His hands were tied with a rope, and Fuenfkorn drove him along in front of them like a calf. That was something!

Gayer was thrown into the jail. The three others went into the house. I was right behind them. Perhaps I could learn something. All three sat down in the kitchen. They seemed to be thirsty. Frederika had to get cider out of the cellar. I wasn't chased away.

"You can sit down here with us," Uncle invited me.

Then the secret policeman reported briefly and tersely:

"There's a tavern called By the Linden in Laemmersbach. Figured it played a role in the robberies. Proceeded systematically. First interrogated both victims, under ox drover and Bofinger. Found out that both had been in the Linden the days before they were held up. Both had mentioned something about the money there. Logically, I had to research who could have heard that. So all present at the Linden went under the magnifying glass, as we police say. Three were possibilities. Observed all three. Gayer made himself particularly suspect. Needed only a corpus delicti, as we police say.

The little Knapp girl helped me there. Nabbed her on the way to school, so that Gayer wouldn't see. After much questioning she recollected something. She slept poorly at night out of fear. Always heard when Gayer came home. And each time Gayer climbed up to the hayloft. Then a trunk lid or something like that slammed shut. Well, then. The rest is obvious."

Uncle and the secret policeman, carrying a heavy sack on his shoulder, went into the office. Now they would have to write down everything in an official report. But what could be in the sack?

Frederika slid back and forth on the stove bench with curiosity.

"Fuenfkorn," she asked ingratiatingly, "wouldn't you like another cider?" She knew when she asked that he never said no to cider. He took a few mighty swallows, and then he told it almost by himself. Frederika only needed to keep pouring.

"So, we went to Schoenbronn. I, the mayor, and the secret policeman. Frau Gayer wondered about the important visitors. She even offered us some homemade pear brandy, because she never imagined it was a criminal matter. She took it for a friendly visit of honorables. She really didn't know anything about what was going on. Gayer himself was as hasty and hostile as always and as nervous as a goose sitting on eggs. The mayor didn't dance about long. He told Gayer that he was there in an official capacity and that he, Gayer, was not permitted to leave. We went straight to the hayloft. There lay three bundles of straw and a few old potato sacks. The mayor looked around, but the secret policeman went straight to the potato sacks, shoved them aside, and what do you think we saw?"

Beadle and Police Constable Fuenfkorn took time out for a gulp of cider.

"The chest!" said Frederika and I at the same time.

"Right!" Fuenfkorn continued. "So there was an old chest. With a big lock. Gayer was asked if he had the key. He went dead pale and said he'd never seen the chest before. The previous owner of the farm must have left the old thing. No, of course he, Gayer, didn't have the key to it. The mayor said more than a little loudly that he wasn't going to be made an ass of. He said 'made an ass of,' so you could see how angry the mayor was and that Gayer had even gotten on his nerves. The mayor told me to look for a crowbar or something like that to break open the lid. Whereupon Frau Gayer said that wouldn't be necessary and that she would get the key because her husband had put it under the mattress. She went right off to get it and her husband shouted after his old woman that she was a dumb cow. Frau Gayer came with the key. She opened the old chest. And what do you think was in it?"

Cider break.

"You'd never guess. On top lay a big black hat. Just like the one that Robber Knapp usually wears. Under it lay a black kerchief for a face mask, and under that a pistol and two heavy money belts, crammed full. At first Frau Gayer didn't know what was going on. She never was particularly smart, you know. So why should she be today? It didn't dawn on her until we were tying her husband up with rope, and then she got big saucer eyes like a newborn calf, and she screamed and cried her heart out. The corpora delic … whatchemacallits are in the sack they took into the mayor's office. Now we only have to ask the under ox drover and Bofinger if those are their money belts. *Exakt!* What am I doing sitting around here! I'm still supposed to get both of them today!"

And with quick steps he hurried away.

"Oh-god-oh-god-oh-god!" said Frederika. More she couldn't say. It took a while before the second sentence came. "And such a respectable, well-to-do farmer, Gayer!"

Something else occurred to me.

"Frederika!" I said excitedly. "Then Knapp is entirely innocent! I have to tell Christian quick. He'll be so happy. And Karolyn doesn't have to stay at the Gayer farm anymore."

The Harvest

EVERYTHING HAPPENED as everything must.

"Of course Knapp is innocent, but he must still be considered a robber!" That's just what Herr Senior Clerk in Backnang told my uncle.

"Mayor Schroll," he said. "A flea is a flea, and whether it bites or not is completely irrelevant. Knapp was a robber for twelve months and so he remains one. His criminal record is long enough without the holdups of the under ox drover and Bofinger."

My uncle respectfully asked what kind of a criminal record might that be, then, and Herr Senior Clerk answered him kindly and graciously.

"It's a long list, my dear mayor!" he'd said. "For example there are disobedience and insubordination to servants of the authorities; light-minded roaming about without employment; vagrancy; noncompliance with official orders; unau-

thorized sleeping in the forest; removal of wood; unauthorized removal of water from springs; unauthorized hunting;
and so forth and so on. And besides it must not and cannot
be that a robber who was on the most-wanted list for a whole
year can suddenly be an innocent man. He has even insulted
the Crown Prince himself. Not directly, of course, but nevertheless . . . He led an entire company of his regiment around
by the nose and made them look foolish and would not allow
himself to be caught. One can't simply let that go. Royal soldiers aren't just puppets, after all. Robber Knapp has made
us a laughingstock in the entire kingdom. And this rogue
should all of a sudden not be a robber anymore? Really, that
just won't do at all."

My uncle then raised the subject of his saving me. "Without Knapp my nephew would most certainly have frozen to
death."

But this effort, too, was in vain.

To that Herr Senior Clerk replied: "Something like that is
no heroic act. That is the most obvious Christian duty."

Now my uncle had used up his last ammunition.

"The law has neither heart nor mercy!" Uncle summed
up his vain petition to Herr Senior Clerk in Backnang.
"There is not one spark of Christian charity in these people."

Nevertheless, some things changed in the village.

The church convention and the village council decided on
the same day that Frau Knapp should have her children
back. Gottfried Knapp wanted to stay with the Weberbauers
in Morbach. It was good for him there, and they treated him
like their own child. Christian wanted to keep on living with

us. The only bed in the poorhouse was much too small. Frau
Knapp would become a maid at our place. She was responsible for the barn and for milking ten cows in the evening. For
that she got enough for food and clothing for herself,
Karolyn, and Wilhelmine.

I was content with God. There was nothing to object to in
the way He had treated the village of Graab. I hadn't felt so
good in a year and a half. Uncle liked me more and more
from day to day. Even a true father couldn't be much better.
Frederika had been a loving mother from the very beginning. And if I thought about it carefully, Christian and
Karolyn were like brother and sister to me. What more
did I want? No, I wanted nothing more. It should stay the
way it was.

The days sped past and suddenly it was time for two
weeks' vacation for the grain harvest. The spelt and barley
were ripe. They stood tall and golden yellow in the fields.
The oats and corn still needed some more time. But if you
waited too long for the spelt and barley, a hailstorm might
come and beat it down. It wouldn't be the first time that
everything was destroyed at the last minute. Or the grains
would fall by themselves if they weren't harvested in time.

A dry, blue, high-summer sky arched over the village. All
morning the birds sang in a mixed choir. In the afternoon
they were too lazy to do it, because it was hot.

The overlong work-filled days had arrived. At home we
slept only a short time. From breakfast till supper everything
took place in the fields. The men mowed. They thrust the
scythes along the ground into the wheat. Beautifully and

evenly the stalks fell to the side. Maids and children made
manageable bundles out of them, bound them into sheaves,
and set up shocks. Everyone worked from the first beam of
sunlight until the evening dusk.

Betweentimes, the children cooled themselves in the lake,
and in the evenings they washed off the straw dust. The
water bubbled and boiled with the hundredfold bodies in
the lake. The boys went into the water in their trousers. The
girls were decorously covered in their pinafores, and there
was much laughter when in deeper water pinafores floated
to the top.

Ꞩow ꝈꞮꝼꞫ Ꞩs

THE BLACK DEVIL'S CAT hadn't been seen again for weeks.

The summer slowly turned into fall. On some mornings fog hung like a dingy milk soup or like a thick spider web over the village.

On such a half-summer, half-fall day we did the second haying in the lake field. My hands didn't blister anymore. They were already used to the work. I was always raking behind Uncle—fast and rhythmically so that the distance between us never got any wider. The hay crunched almost dry, and it smelled strongly of the summer herbs. Suddenly my uncle stopped, lifted his scythe, turned to me, and waited until I came up to him. Then he looked me direct in the face for what seemed a long time.

I knew that he was going to say something very serious and important to me. I already knew him that well.

Nevertheless I was surprised. He spoke quietly and calmly. "Frankly, I'm fed up with your calling me Uncle all the time. Think of something else."

And because I couldn't conceal my surprise, I probably looked as stupid as the farmhand did when he secretly stole from the jam jar and instead of a sweet treat popped into his mouth some of the herb mixture Frederika had concocted for her varicose veins.

"You'll think of something," Uncle said a little disappointedly after a while. Then he went on mowing the hay and I kept standing there thinking. What should I call him? I really couldn't call him Emil. I would have preferred Father. Perhaps that was what he meant, or perhaps he meant something else altogether. If only I knew!

So at first I'd say nothing. I'd ask Frederika.

Only rarely did I remember anymore that I was an orphan.

Then suddenly the black Devil's cat was in the village again.

Of course it was all foolishness and obviously only a coincidence. But just one day after that damned animal turned up again, it happened.

Very early in the morning—it was practically still night—Frederika came into our bedroom. I didn't really notice why she came and what she wanted because I was very sleepy and dropped right off again.

Shortly thereafter I was awakened again. It was still more night than day. There was a busy clamor in the yard that spoiled my sleep. Horses were clattering unwillingly out of the barn, the bull was pulling on the chain, and the rooster began to crow early. The young farmhand was cursing like a godless apprentice from the city. Why was he taking the light wagon out of the carriage shed at such an early hour? Probably he had an errand to Hall, Heilbronn, or even to Stuttgart. Out of curiosity I went to the window. Above Schoenbronn I could make out a small stripe of daylight in the sky. Daniel was standing beside the jail with the stable lantern. It improved the weak daylight from the east.

Uncle came out of the house. He spoke quietly with the young hand. Out of the twilight emerged Beadle and Police Constable Fuenfkorn. He stalked up in full uniform.

"Reporting for duty!" he announced in front of the mayor's house.

"Don't be so loud!" the mayor chided him.

Christian was sound asleep, as always. You could carry him away without his even noticing. In any event, the noise down below didn't bother him.

I went over to the bed. "Hey, Christian!" I said. "Something's going on downstairs. Come to the window! Even Fuenfkorn is up and about this early. That's rare. Something's going to happen soon down there!"

Christian didn't move. Should I wake him? If I didn't he would miss whatever it was that was happening down in the yard in the middle of the night. It had to be worth seeing!

"Wake up, Christian!" I said somewhat louder, and I felt around in the bed.

To my surprise, Christian wasn't there!

"Hey, Christian," I said, "where are you?"

Perhaps he'd only gone to the toilet without my noticing it on account of the noise down below. Certainly he'd be right back.

I returned to the window and looked down. The hand had hitched up the horses, and they were stamping the ground restlessly. Frederika came out of the house. She had a bundle in her hand.

And right behind her came Christian, completely dressed—in the middle of summer!—with shoes on his feet and his Sunday jacket over his arm. Was he going away? Of course. A person only dresses like that when he's going to the city. Why didn't I know about it?

Frederika pressed the bundle into his hand, took his head between her great hands, and kissed him somewhere on the face. A sliver of ice pierced my chest, and I knew that Christian was going away for a long time. Maybe forever.

I didn't think about anything else at all. I just leapt down the stairs and in a moment was standing in front of Christian. He laid the bundle in the wagon, came up to me, and pressed my head to his.

Frederika said something, then said something else—I don't remember what—and then she pulled me away. "You'll catch the gout," she scolded, "if you stand around naked like that."

Then I noticed that I had nothing on.

Just then Robber Knapp came up with his wife, and there,

too, were little Wilhelmine, Gottfried, and Karolyn with the long braid down to her behind.

I was ashamed to stand in front of Karolyn because I was naked. Did I see Robber Knapp smiling?

I ran right up the stairs. I was utterly confused. Where were my trousers and shirt?

Karolyn was going away too. All the Knapps were going away! And now again I hadn't seen Robber Knapp properly, only his smile. And I hadn't thanked him still for saving me from freezing to death.

Down in the courtyard I heard Uncle and Fuenfkorn. *"Exakt!"* he commanded and the wagon drove off. The hand was driving. His voice was unmistakable. *"Hu!"* he cried to the horses. The vehicle clattered away over the crushed stone of the road.

Where were my trousers? I crept around over the floor feeling for my clothes.

In my throat there was something the size of a plum, and my chest was as heavy as a wheat sack.

I could have looked forever on the floor, since my trousers were hanging on a nail in the rafter. I slithered into them and ran down the stairs again. Only Frederika and Fuenfkorn were standing there in the yard.

"Where are they?"

"They've gone already."

I ran down the village street. It was still before dawn. In front of the schoolmaster's house I stepped in the liquid manure ditch. The stinking brew splashed up on my nose

and cheeks. Then I was standing at the crossing. Where had
they gone? In this direction or that one? I strained to hear.
Somewhere there was the sound of iron wheels on the stones.
But where was it?

Then I knew that I could no longer catch up to the
Knapps.

"You can cry," said Frederika when I came back to
the mayor's house and she saw my wet face.

"I'm not crying!" I answered angrily. "That's just
manure."

Then Frederika laughed fondly and took her apron and
wiped my face clean.

The wheat sack fell away from my chest, and even the
plum in my throat got smaller. How glad I was that there
was a Frederika!

Uncle was sitting in the kitchen, and all the others
were there too, except for the young hand. Uncle said to
Frederika that it would probably be best if we had something to eat right away, for there certainly wouldn't be any
more sleep that night, and eating kept body and soul together. "Especially the soul," he repeated, and he looked at
me as he said it.

Frederika was already busy about the stove. She put
dry twigs on the embers, blew hard on them, and the fire in
the stove crackled. The heavens were showing through the
kitchen window. The sky was clear, and it was getting
lighter and lighter from Schoenbronn toward us.

"That's how life is," said Uncle after a while. "People

come and people go." And because I looked at him question-ingly, he added, "It's the best thing for the Knapps. They're emigrating to America."

"Why so suddenly?" I asked.

"It just happened that way. The faster, the better. Then no one gets any foolish ideas. And besides, it's better for the rob-ber to be gone before the superior judge in Backnang learns of his emigration plans."

"Oh!" I sighed, and then I went up to my room without any breakfast. I didn't want to bawl in front of Uncle and Frederika and Daniel and the under maids.

But up there I saw the empty bed. That was even worse. I was already missing Christian. How would it be by evening and at night? With whom would I talk everything over before going to sleep? And in the next thunderstorm I'd be alone with my fear. Christian wouldn't crowd up close to make the fear go away.

Karolyn with the beautiful long braid was also gone. When I closed my eyes I saw her beautiful face, or saw her splashing with the other children in the lake and her pina-fore floating on the water.

I wiped my eyes dry and then I went back down to the kitchen. Frederika placed a pot of malt coffee in front of me and spread a piece of bread with butter for me. Uncle said that he had to go to Oberrot today, and he needed me with him. Frederika nodded her head. They both always knew what was just the right thing.

The Birthday Present

ONE MORNING not long after that there was a gigantic, golden-yellow braid of yeast bread on the table at breakfast. Without it being Sunday or a holiday.

Frederika said that maybe it had been baked just for me. She had put eight eggs in it, she said, so that it would taste especially good, and she had almost not been able to get it into the oven, it was so big.

For me? I wondered. Something didn't fit here, and there were a few riddles twisting in my head. You didn't always know what was what with the people in the mayor's house.

When Uncle came in, I found out. He was cheerfully serious, or as good-humoredly respectful as he was with Herr Senior Clerk from Backnang when he had drunk two steins of pear cider with him.

He congratulated me very seriously, and all just because I was twelve years old today. Of course he did it in his reserved, semiofficial way. But by now I knew that he meant it very differently. He was just the kind of man who kept his heart well hidden.

There was also a festive meal at midday, and I imagined how nice it would be to have several birthdays.

After supper and the work in the barn, Uncle said he wanted to see how things were in the Fritz field and that it would be a good thing if I went with him. That was the second time that my uncle devoted himself to me alone. Only to me.

Traces of daylight were still showing in the sky in the west; in the east, the first stars had already appeared over Schoenbronn.

"You can ask for something for your birthday!" he said. At the same time he pulled up a handful of potato greens and checked the tuber at the end of them.

I was startled. My birthday had been celebrated only once in my life, so far as I could remember. That was the year my father gave me one of those new pencils and a package of paper. Aunt Wilhelmine had never thought about my birthday. Maybe she didn't even know that I'd been born.

"For example, it could be a knife, or a book," said Uncle. "There's a new one by a Frenchman, a fellow named Jules Verne. *Journey to the Center of the Earth* it's called. And it's not just a schoolbook, I hear, but very exciting."

I stopped in my tracks, I was so happy.

"Do you know what you want, Boniface? But there's no hurry, you can think it over if you want."

I just stood there.

My own book! That would be wonderful! Or a knife!

But there wasn't really anything to think over. I knew exactly what I wanted him to give me.

"Uncle," I said, "I don't want a knife, and I don't want a book either. I want you to throw me way up in the air and catch me again."

Silence.

Nothing!

Was it wrong what I asked for? Perhaps I ought not to have said it. Already disappointment was creeping over me, and I was beginning to feel ashamed of my request. How could I wish for something so childish. At twelve years old!

Then Uncle grabbed me very quickly by the hips and tossed me into the air. I got quite dizzy, I flew up so high.

I hung there a while between heaven and earth. Then I fell back down to Uncle, and I lay firmly grasped in his arms.

I just lay there. Uncle didn't move either. More and more stars came out. The red stripe in the west disappeared into the forest.

I let go of Uncle and jumped down into the meadow.

"You know what, Uncle? I've had enough of calling you Uncle all the time. Have you anything against my calling you Father?"

Translator's Note

IN 1867, when Boniface's story takes place, Germany was still a few years away from becoming the nation we recognize today. Instead there was a confederation of kingdoms, each governed by its own ruler. The most powerful of these was Prussia, under whose leadership the German states unified to become the German Empire after the Franco-Prussian War in 1870–71. In Wuerttemberg, where the novel is set, the king governed with the help of an assembly of representatives elected by propertied citizens, and the Lutheran Church had a powerful voice in the affairs of the country as well. As Boniface points out, the king was considered God's representative, and so he was able to govern with a firm hand. Democracy as we think of it was only a dream in the minds of radicals and rebels, many of whom chose to emigrate to find the freedom they believed to be every man's right. For those born into the poorest working classes, like the farmhands and the day laborers, there was also almost no honest way to improve their living conditions except to emigrate (or to sell their souls to the Devil for a chest of gold!), so great numbers of people left Germany for the United States during the 1850s and 1860s. Germany's loss was America's gain.

If you look on a map for the places mentioned in this story, you won't find a village called Graab, but you can probably figure out just about where the author imagines it. Cannstatt is a real place, an ancient Roman crossroads that was chartered as a city in the Middle Ages. Lying northeast of Stuttgart, it became a part of that city in 1905 and so does not appear on modern maps. You can find Ludwigsburg, Heilbronn, Schwaebisch Hall (called Hall in the story), Mergentheim, Backnang, Salzbach, Murrhardt, and Gaildorf, and somewhere to the north of Murrhardt and south of Hall, east of Salzbach and west of Gaildorf, in the forested area on the map that is empty of names is where you can picture the village of Graab.

Finally, I want to say a word about the way German words are spelled in this book. As you may have noticed, I've avoided using those characteristic two little dots over certain vowels, called the umlaut (which literally means a "change of sound"). The umlaut always indicates that the two vowel sounds are combined and so are changed into another (called a "diphthong"), and sometimes that change also changes the meaning of the word. Hoping to make reading easier, I've used the actual vowels instead of the umlaut. On maps, for example, you won't see *Schwaebisch* but *Schwäbisch*, or

Wuerttemberg but *Württemberg*, and though you won't find *Boehringswilder* on any map, if you did, it would be written *Böhringswilder*. When a word should be spelled with an umlaut, it is an actual misspelling not to use the symbol or somehow show that there is a change of sound.

—E. D. C.

Glossary

BEADLE   A herald or messenger, especially in the service of a law court.

CONSISTORY   An administrative body appointed by the civil authority to administer affairs in Lutheran state churches.

CONSUMPTION   An older name for the disease tuberculosis.

CONVENTION   A church governing body, with the minister, elders, and perhaps some members of the congregation.

CORPUS DELICTI   Latin for "the body of the crime"— meaning, the evidence.

DREI [dry]   Here used as a name, but also the German word for the number "three."

EXAKT   German for "precisely," "absolutely."

FRAU   German for "Mrs."; hence, Robber Knapp's wife is Frau Knapp.

GENDARME   A rural policeman.

GOUT   An extremely painful disease that affects the joints and today is known to be diet-related; it may be that people in the story really mean rheumatism when they talk of gout.

GULDEN   A gold coin.

HERR   German for "Mister"; often used before a person's title as a sign of respect, as in Herr Captain, or Herr Schoolmaster.

KREUZER [*kroyt*-zer]   A small coin, like a penny.

OEHMD [ehrmd]   Hay from the second cutting.

POACHER   A person who takes fish or game without permission; since the forests and their contents belonged to the king, it was illegal for ordinary people to fish, hunt, or cut wood.

QUINSY   Old-fashioned name for an abscess around the
tonsils.

SPAETZLE [*shpetz*-leh]   A kind of noodle.

SPELT   A type of wheat, not grown in United States but
common in Germany.